THIS BOOK
BELONGS TO:

GOLDILOCKS
AND THE
THREE BEARS
AND OTHER CLASSIC ENGLISH FAIRY TALES

CHILDREN'S CLASSICS

This unique series of Children's Classics™ features accessible and highly readable texts paired with the work of talented and brilliant illustrators of bygone days to create fine editions for today's parents and children to rediscover and treasure. Besides being a handsome addition to any home library, this series features genuine bonded-leather spines stamped in gold, full-color illustrations, and high-quality acid-free paper that will enable these books to be passed from one generation to the next.

Adventures of Huckleberry Finn
The Adventures of Tom Sawyer
Aesop's Fables
Alice's Adventures in Wonderland
Andersen's Fairy Tales
Anne of Avonlea
Anne of Green Gables
At the Back of the North Wind
Black Beauty
The Call of the Wild
A Child's Book of Country Stories
A Child's Book of Stories
A Child's Book of Stories from
    Many Lands
A Child's Christmas
A Christmas Carol and Other
    Christmas Stories
Cinderella and Other Classic Italian
    Fairy Tales
The Complete Mother Goose
Goldilocks and the Three Bears and
    Other Classic English Fairy Tales
Great Dog Stories
Grimm's Fairy Tales
Hans Brinker *or* The Silver Skates
Heidi

The Hound of the Baskervilles
The Jungle Book
Just So Stories
Kidnapped
King Arthur and His Knights
A Little Child's Book of Stories
Little Men
The Little Princess
Little Women
Peter Pan
Rebecca of Sunnybrook Farm
Robin Hood
Robinson Crusoe
The Secret Garden
The Sleeping Beauty and Other
    Classic French Fairy Tales
The Swiss Family Robinson
Tales from Shakespeare
Tales of Pirates and Buccaneers
Through the Looking Glass and
    What Alice Found There
Treasure Island
A Very Little Child's Book of
    Stories
The Wind in the Willows

GOLDILOCKS
AND THE
THREE BEARS
AND OTHER CLASSIC ENGLISH FAIRY TALES

Retold by Flora Annie Steel
Edited and with an Introduction by
Christine Messina

Illustrated by
Arthur Rackham and Jessie Willcox Smith

CHILDREN'S CLASSICS
New York • Avenel

This edition is published by Children's Classics, a division of dilithium Press, Ltd., distributed by Random House Value Publishing, Inc., 40 Engelhard Avenue, Avenel, New Jersey 07001.

DILITHIUM is a registered trademark and CHILDREN'S CLASSICS is a trademark of dilithium Press, Ltd.

Random House
New York · Toronto · London · Sydney · Auckland

Printed and bound in the United States of America

Library of Congress Cataloging-in-Publication Data

Steel, Flora Annie Webster, 1847–1929.
    Goldilocks and the three bears and other classic English fairy tales / retold by Flora Annie
Steel; edited, with an introduction by Christina Messina.
        p.   cm.
    Summary: Presents a collection of both familiar and lesser-known English fairy tales,
including "Tattercoats," and "Jack and the Beanstalk."
    ISBN 0–517–10176–9
    1. Fairy tales—England. [1. Fairy tales. 2. Folklore—England.] I. Messina, Christina.
PZ8.S53Go   1994
398.21—dc20   93-44688
                                                                                   CIP
                                                                                    AC

Front cover illustration: "Goldilocks" by Jessie Willcox Smith
Back cover illustration: "The Three Bears" by Arthur Rackham

Cover design by Don Bender
Production supervision by Roméo Enriquez
Editorial supervision by Claire Booss

8   7   6   5   4   3   2

CONTENTS

Contents

LIST OF COLOR ILLUSTRATIONS

PREFACE TO
THIS ILLUSTRATED EDITION

IN THE FIRST quarter of the twentieth century, Flora Annie Steel gathered these delightful tales into a collection she titled *English Fairy Tales*. Fortunately for her readers, Arthur Rackham was commissioned to create humorous and engaging line drawings to appear throughout the text, as well as entrancing full-page color illustrations for many of the stories.

For this Children's Classics edition, these treasures from the past have been retrieved, and in addition, there are two lovely paintings by Jessie Willcox Smith—her lively picture of Jack and the famous beanstalk, and her vision of Goldilocks sampling the porridge of the Three Bears, a charming complement to Arthur Rackham's scene showing the bears' discovery that the porridge is missing.

CLAIRE BOOSS
Series Editor

1994

Acknowledgment

The publishers of this edition would like to thank Donna Lee Lurker for helpful editorial consultation on the stories chosen for this collection.

INTRODUCTION

"Someone has been in lying my bed," said the Little Wee Bear, "and she's still there!"

ALMOST EVERY English-speaking person remembers that sentence. And we all learned its lesson: Don't fall asleep in a strange bed, no matter how comfortable it is. The story of *Goldilocks and the Three Bears* has been told for more than two hundred years. (The actual moral: Don't poke around in other people's—or for that matter, other bears'—houses.) But when Goldilocks first appeared in print in the 1830s, her hair wasn't gold. And she wasn't a little girl, but a little old lady. That is the way an Englishwoman named Eleanor Mure first told the story in 1831, when she wrote it down for her young nephew. A few years later, in 1837, another writer, Robert Southey, made the story famous when he published it in a book of essays called *The Doctor.*

After many tellings and retellings, the old woman was replaced with an overcurious little girl. And thus, at first, this child was named "Silver-Hair." Years later, her hair had turned to gold, and the name "Goldilocks," by which most of us know her today, was first used in *Old Nursery Stories and Rhymes,* which was published around 1904.

Introduction

All of the different versions of *Goldilocks* have different endings. Sometimes that naughty girl runs off into the woods and simply disappears; in others she comes home, tells her mother what happened, and promises to behave herself in the future. Eleanor Mure punished the old woman (later to become Goldilocks) by first tossing her on a bonfire and then throwing her up into the steeple of St. Paul's. Gradually, through many tellings, the story changed until it became the story we know and love today.

The version you will read here is unique because it is told from the point of view of the bears—three "well-brought-up" bears, who unexpectedly have a spoiled, rude little girl named Goldilocks as their uninvited guest. This version, and all of the other tales in this delightful book, come from *English Fairy Tales*, collected and retold by Flora Annie Steel in England in the early twentieth century.

The tradition of the fairy tale exists in all countries and all languages. In America, we inherited the English fairy tale along with the English language. And American parents born in other countries tell their children fairy tales that originated in the lands of their heritage. Still, despite some differences in details, many fairy tales are almost the same from one country to another.

English fairy tales do not seem as fantastical as the stories that originated in France, Italy, and the Orient. Although they have plenty of witches and giants and occasional magic tricks, these stories, for the most part, are as real as can be. They are often-told tales of boys and girls fallen on hard times, abandoned or otherwise badly treated by their parents, and misunderstood by those they meet in the course of their adventures. No matter how dejected and miserable they are made by their circumstances, they manage to overcome adversity by wit and bravery. The clever ways they achieve success are at the heart of every tale. Often it is their own resourcefulness that saves the day; however, when things are very bad indeed, magic is sometimes required to rescue them.

In some of these tales messages are hidden. The message may be a simple one: A poor, lonely old lady in *The Bogey Beast*, for example, sees only goodness and luck, no matter how dismal her situation. Other stories are episodic and complex. *Jack the Giant-Killer* is a young man who lusts for adventure, traveling from kingdom to kingdom, using his wits and daring exploits to dispatch one giant after another. *Jack and the Beanstalk*, one of the most famous stories in English literature, appears here in its classic version. The giant's pronouncement, "Fee Fi Fo Fum. I smell the blood of an Englishman!" echoes down the pages of history.

A class attitude pervades English fairy tales. Being poor is frowned upon. The poor are bad; the rich and noble are good. This strong aversion to poverty can be traced back to Arthurian legends. The code of chivalry, which means "cavalry," originated in the Arthurian period. Only medieval knights rode horses; serfs fought on foot and were called "infantry." The English phrase "cavalier fashion" describes the callousness with which gentlemen upon their horses treated the so-called lower classes, a division implicit in the Arthurian tales.

What was different about the fairy tales—as opposed to real

Introduction

life in those times—was that people could change their lives. If a poor lad or lass was clever enough and enterprising enough, he or she could gain a fortune and marry into a noble family.

The desire for happiness and the surmounting of obstacles were born in these tales, which contain the seeds of English literature.

CHRISTINE MESSINA

New York City
1994

GOLDILOCKS
AND THE
THREE BEARS
AND OTHER CLASSIC ENGLISH FAIRY TALES

GOLDILOCKS AND THE THREE BEARS

ONCE upon a time there were Three Bears, who lived together in a house of their own, in a wood. One of them was a Little Wee Bear, one was a Middle-sized Bear, and the other was a Great Big Bear. They each had a bowl for their porridge: a little wee bowl for the Little Wee Bear, a middle-sized bowl for the Middle-sized Bear, and a great big bowl for the Great Big Bear. And they each had a chair to sit in: a little wee chair for the Little Wee Bear, a middle-sized chair for the Middle-sized Bear, and a great big chair for the Great Big Bear. And they each had a bed to sleep in: a little wee bed for the Little Wee Bear, a middle-sized bed for the Middle-sized Bear, and a great big bed for the Great Big Bear.

One day, after they had made the porridge for their breakfast, and poured it into their porridge bowls, they walked out into the wood while the porridge was cooling, so they would not burn their mouths by beginning to eat too soon, for they were polite, well-brought-up bears. And while they were away a little girl called Goldilocks, who lived on the other side of the wood and had been sent on an errand by her mother, passed by the house, and looked in the window. And then she peeped in at the keyhole, for

1

she was not at all a well-brought-up little girl. Then, seeing nobody in the house, she lifted the latch. The door was not fastened, because the bears were good bears, who did nobody any harm, and never suspected that anybody would harm them. So Goldilocks opened the door and went in. She was very pleased when she saw the porridge on the table. If she had been a well-brought-up little girl she would have waited till the bears came home, and then, perhaps, they would have asked her to breakfast, for they were good bears—a little rough, as is the manner of bears, but, for all that, very good-natured and hospitable. But she was an impudent, rude little girl, and so she set about helping herself.

First she tasted the porridge of the Great Big Bear, and that was too hot for her. Next she tasted the porridge of the Middle-sized Bear, but that was too cold for her. And then she went to the porridge of the Little Wee Bear, and tasted it, and that was neither too hot nor too cold, but just right, and she liked it so much that she ate it all up, every bit!

Then Goldilocks, who was tired, for she had been catching butterflies instead of running on her errand, sat down in the chair of the Great Big Bear, but that was too hard for her. And then she sat down in the chair of the Middle-sized Bear, and that was too soft for her. But when she sat down in the chair of the Little Wee Bear, that was neither too hard nor too soft, but just right. So she seated herself in it, and there she sat till the bottom of the chair came out, and down she came, plump upon the ground; and that made her very cross, for she was a bad-tempered little girl.

Goldilocks and the Three Bears

Now, being determined to rest, Goldilocks went upstairs into the bedroom in which the Three Bears slept. And first she lay down upon the bed of the Great Big Bear, but that was too high at the head for her. And next she lay down upon the bed of the Middle-sized Bear, and that was too high at the foot for her. And then she lay down upon the bed of the Little Wee Bear, and that was neither too high at the head nor at the foot, but just right. So she covered herself up comfortably, and lay there till she fell fast asleep.

By this time the Three Bears thought their porridge would be cool enough for them to eat, so they came home to breakfast. But, careless Goldilocks had left the spoon of the Great Big Bear standing in his porridge.

"SOMEBODY HAS BEEN AT MY PORRIDGE!"

said the Great Big Bear in his great, rough, gruff voice.

Then the Middle-sized Bear looked at his porridge and saw the spoon was standing in it too.

"SOMEBODY HAS BEEN AT MY PORRIDGE!"

said the Middle-sized Bear in his middle-sized voice.

Then the Little Wee Bear looked at his, and there was the spoon in the porridge bowl, but the porridge was all gone!

"SOMEBODY HAS BEEN AT MY PORRIDGE, AND HAS EATEN IT ALL UP!"

3

said the Little Wee Bear in his little wee voice.

At that, the Three Bears, seeing that someone had entered their house and eaten up the Little Wee Bear's breakfast, began to look about them. Now the careless Goldilocks had not put the cushion straight when she rose from the chair of the Great Big Bear.

"SOMEBODY HAS BEEN SITTING IN MY CHAIR!"

said the Great Big Bear in his great, rough, gruff voice.

And the careless Goldilocks had squashed down the soft cushion of the Middle-sized Bear.

"SOMEBODY HAS BEEN SITTING IN MY CHAIR!"

said the Middle-sized Bear in his middle-sized voice.

"SOMEBODY HAS BEEN SITTING IN MY CHAIR, AND HAS SAT THE BOTTOM THROUGH!"

said the Little Wee Bear in his little wee voice.

Then the Three Bears thought they had better search further in case it was a burglar, so they went upstairs into their bedroom. Now Goldilocks had pulled the pillow of the Great Big Bear out of place.

"SOMEBODY HAS BEEN LYING IN MY BED!"

Goldilocks and the Three Bears

said the Great Big Bear in his great, rough, gruff voice.

And Goldilocks had pulled the bolster of the Middle-sized Bear out of its place.

"SOMEBODY HAS BEEN LYING IN MY BED!"

said the Middle-sized Bear in his middle-sized voice.

But when the Little Wee Bear came to look at his bed, there was the bolster in its place!

And the pillow was in its place upon the bolster!

And upon the pillow—? There was Goldilocks' head—which was not in its place, for she had no business being there.

"SOMEBODY HAS BEEN LYING IN MY BED—AND HERE SHE IS STILL!"

said the Little Wee Bear in his little wee voice.

Goldilocks had heard in her sleep the great, rough, gruff voice of the Great Big Bear; but she was so fast asleep that it was no more to her than the roaring of wind, or the rumbling of thunder. And she had heard the middle-sized voice of the Middle-sized Bear, but it was only as if she had heard someone speaking in a dream. But when she heard the little wee voice of the Little Wee Bear, it was so sharp, and so shrill, that it awakened her at once. Up she started, and when she saw the Three Bears on one side of the bed, she tumbled out on the other, and ran to the window. The window was open, because the bears, like the good, tidy bears that they were, always opened their bedroom window when they got up in the morning. So naughty, frightened little Goldilocks jumped; and whether she

"SOMEBODY HAS BEEN LYING IN MY BED—AND HERE SHE IS!"

broke her ankle in the fall, or ran into the wood and was lost there, or found her way out of the wood and got punished for being selfish and playing truant, no one can say. But the Three Bears never saw anything more of her.

TOM-TIT-TOT

ONCE upon a time there was a woman who baked five pies. But when they came out of the oven they were overbaked, and the crust was far too hard to eat. So she said to her daughter, "Daughter, put them pies on to the shelf and leave them there awhile. Surely they'll come again in time."

By that she meant that the crust would become softer; but her daughter said to herself, "If Mother says the pies will come again, why shouldn't I eat these now?" So, having good, young teeth, she set to work and ate them all, first and last.

When suppertime came, the woman said to her daughter, "Go and get one of the pies. They are sure to have come again by now."

The girl went and looked, but, of course, there was nothing but the empty dishes.

So back she came and said, "No, Mother, they ain't come again."

"Not one of them?" asked the mother, taken aback.

"Not one of them," said the daughter, quite confident.

"Well," said the mother, "come again, or not come again, I will have one of them pies for my supper."

"But you can't," said the daughter. "How can you if they ain't come? And they ain't, as sure's sure."

"But I can," said the mother, getting angry. "Go at once, child, and bring me the best of them. My teeth must try it."

"Best or worst is all one," answered the daughter, quite sulky, "for I've ate them all, so you can't have one till it comes again—so there!"

Well, the mother bounced up to see; but half an eye told her there was nothing but empty dishes; so she was dished up herself and done for.

Having no supper, she took her spinning to the doorstep and began to spin the skeins of yarn. And as she spun, she sang:

> "My daughter has eaten five pies today,
> My daughter has eaten five pies today,
> My daughter has eaten five pies today."

Now the King happened to be riding down the street, and he heard the song going on and on, but could not quite make out the words. So he stopped his horse, and asked "What is that you are singing, my good woman?"

The mother, though horrified at her daughter's appetite, did not want other folk, least of all the King, to know about it, so she sang instead:

> "My daughter has spun five skeins today,
> My daughter has spun five skeins today,
> My daughter has spun five skeins today."

"Five skeins!" cried the King. "By my crown, I never heard tell of anyone who could do that! Look here, I have been

searching for a wife, and your daughter who can spin five skeins a day is the very one for me. Only, mind you, for eleven months of the year she shall be Queen indeed, and have all she likes to eat, all the gowns she likes to wear, all the company she likes to keep, and everything her heart desires, but in the twelfth month she must set to work and spin five skeins a day, and if she does not, she must die. Come! Is it a bargain?"

Well, the mother agreed. She thought what a grand marriage it was for her daughter. And as for the five skeins? Time enough to worry about them when the year ended. There was many a slip between cup and lip and, likely as not, the King would have forgotten all about it by then.

Anyhow, her daughter would be Queen for eleven months. They were married, and for eleven months the bride was as happy as happy could be. She had everything she liked to eat, and all the gowns she liked to wear, all the company she cared to keep, and everything her heart desired. And her husband, the King, was kind as kind could be. But in the tenth month, she began to think of those five skeins and wonder if the King remembered. And in the eleventh month, she began to dream about them as well. But not a word did the King say about them, and she hoped he had forgotten.

However, on the very last day of the eleventh month, the King led her into a room she had never set eyes on before. It had one window, and there was nothing in it but a stool and a spinning wheel.

"Now, my dear," he said kindly, "you will be shut in here tomorrow morning with some food and some flax, and if by evening you have not spun five skeins, your head will come off."

She was very frightened, for she had always been such a lazy girl that she had never learned to spin at all. What was she to do tomorrow with no one to help her? So she just sat down on the stool, and cried and cried and cried until her pretty eyes were all red.

As she sat sobbing and crying she heard a queer little noise at the bottom of the door. At first she thought it was a mouse. Then she thought it must be something knocking.

So she got up and opened the door and what did she see? Why, it was a small, little Imp with a long tail that whisked round and round ever so fast.

"What are you crying for?" said that Imp, making a bow, and twirling its tail so fast that she could scarcely see it.

"What's that to you?" said she, shrinking a bit, for that Imp was very odd indeed.

"Don't look at my tail if you're frightened," it said, smirking. "Look at my toes. Aren't they beautiful?"

And sure enough it had on buckled shoes with high heels and big bows.

She almost forgot about the tail, and wasn't so frightened, and when that Imp asked her again why she was crying, she said, "It won't do any good if I do tell you."

"You don't know that," it said, twirling its tail faster and faster, and sticking out its toes. "Come, tell me, there's a good girl."

"Well," said she, "it can't do any harm if it doesn't do good." So she dried her pretty eyes and told it all about the pies, and the skeins, and everything from first to last.

And then that little Imp nearly burst with laughing. "If that is all, it's easily mended!" it said. "I'll come to your window every morning, take the flax, and bring it back spun into five skeins at night. Come! Shall it be a bargain?"

Now even though she was thoughtless, she said, cautiously, "But what is your pay?"

The Imp twirled its tail so fast you couldn't see it, and stuck out its beautiful toes, and smirked and looked out of the corners of its eyes. "I will give you three chances every night to guess my name, and if you haven't guessed it before the month is up, why"—and it twirled its tail faster and stuck out its toes further, and sniggered more than ever—"you shall be mine, my beauty."

Three guesses every night for a whole month! She felt sure she would be able to guess its name before the month was up, and so she said, "Yes! I agree!"

And, goodness! How that Imp twirled its tail, and bowed, and smirked, and stuck out its beautiful toes.

The very next day her husband led her to the strange room again, and there was the day's food, and a spinning wheel and a great bundle of flax.

"There you are, my dear," he said politely. "And remember! If there are not five whole skeins tonight, I fear your head will come off!"

At that she began to tremble, and after he had gone away and locked the door, she was ready for a good cry, when she heard a knocking at the window. She opened it at once, and sure enough there was the small, little Imp sitting on the window ledge, dangling its beautiful toes and twirling its tail so fast that you could scarcely see it.

"Good morning, my beauty," said the Imp. "Come! Hand over the flax, there's a good girl."

So she gave it the flax and shut the window and, you may be sure, ate her food, for, as you know, she had a good appetite, and the King had promised to give her everything she liked to eat. So she ate to her heart's content, and when evening came and she heard that knocking at the window again, she opened it, and there was the small, little Imp with five spun skeins on his arm! It twirled its tail faster than ever, and stuck out its beautiful toes, and bowed and smirked and gave her the five skeins.

Then the Imp said, "And now, my beauty, what is my name?"

And she answered quite at ease, "Your name is Bill."

"No, it isn't," said the Imp and twirled its tail.

"Then it is Ned," said she.

"No, it isn't," said the Thing.

"Well," said she, a bit more slowly, "it is Mark."

"No, it isn't," said the Imp, and laughed and laughed and laughed, and twirled its tail so fast that you couldn't see it, and away it flew.

Well, when her husband, the King, came in, he was pleased to see the five skeins all ready for him, for he was fond of his pretty wife.

"I shall not have to order your head off, my dear," said he. "And I hope all the other days will pass as happily." Then he said good night and locked the door and left her.

The next morning they brought her fresh flax and even more delicious foods. And the small, little Imp came knocking at the window and stuck out its beautiful toes and twirled its tail faster and faster, and took away the bundle of flax and brought it back all spun into five skeins by evening. Then the Imp made her guess its name three times, but she could not guess right, and the Imp laughed and laughed and laughed as it flew away.

Now every morning and evening the same thing happened, and every evening she had her three guesses, but she never guessed right. And every day the small, little Imp laughed louder and louder and smirked more and more, and looked at her maliciously out of the corners of its eyes until she began to get frightened, and instead of eating all the fine foods left for her, spent the day trying to think of names to say. But she never hit upon the right one.

So when it came to the last day of the month but one, and when the small, little Imp arrived in the evening with the five skeins of flax already spun, it could hardly contain itself.

"Haven't you got my name yet?" it asked.

So she said, "Is it Nicodemus?"

"No, it isn't," said the Imp, and twirled its tail faster than you could see.

"Is it Samuel?" said she all aflutter.

"No, it isn't, my beauty," chuckled the Imp.

"Well, is it Methuselah?" said she, ready to cry.

Then the Imp looked at her with eyes like fiery coals, and said, "No, it isn't that either, so there is only tomorrow night and then you'll be mine, my beauty."

And away the small, little Imp flew, its tail twirling and whisking so fast that you couldn't see it.

Well, she felt so bad she couldn't even cry. But when she heard the King coming to the door, she tried to be cheerful, and smiled when he said, "Well done, wife! Five skeins again! I shall not have to order your head off after all, my dear, of that I'm quite sure, so let us enjoy ourselves." Then he bade the servants bring supper, and a stool for him to sit beside his Queen, and down they sat side by side.

But the poor Queen could eat nothing; she could not forget the small, little Imp. And the King hadn't eaten but a mouthful or two when he began to laugh, and he laughed so long and so loud that at last the poor Queen said, "Why do you laugh so?"

"At something I saw today, my love," said the King. "I was out hunting, and by chance I came to a place I'd never been in before. It was in a wood, and there was an old chalk pit there, and out of the chalk pit there came a queer kind of a sort of a humming noise. So I got off my horse and went quietly to the edge of the pit and looked down. And what do you think I saw? The funniest, smallest, little Imp you ever set eyes upon. And it had a little spinning wheel and it was spinning away for dear life, but the wheel didn't go so fast as its tail, that spun round and round—*ho-ho-ha-ha!*—you never saw the like. And its little feet had buckled shoes and bows on them, and they went up and down in a desperate hurry. And all the time that small, little Imp kept humming and booming away at these words:

> "Name me, name me not,
>   Who'll guess it's Tom-Tit-Tot."

When she heard these words the Queen nearly jumped out of her skin for joy, but she managed to say nothing, and ate her supper quite comfortably.

She said no word when next morning the small, little Imp came for the flax, though it looked so gleeful and full of malice that she could hardly help laughing. And when night came and she heard that knocking against the window panes, she opened the window slowly as if she was afraid. But that Imp was as bold as brass and came right inside, grinning from ear to ear. And oh, my goodness! How its tail was twirling and whisking!

"Well, my beauty," said the Imp, giving her the five skeins already spun, "what's my name?"

Then she lowered her lip, and said, tearfully, "Is—is—it—Solomon?"

"No, it isn't," laughed the Imp, smirking out of the corner of its eye. And the small, little Imp came further into the room.

So she tried again—and this time she seemed hardly able to speak for fright.

"Well—is it—Zebedee?" she said.

"No, it isn't," cried the imp, full of glee. And it came quite close and stretched out its little hands to her, and O-oh, ITS TAIL . . . !!!

"Take your time, my beauty," said the Imp, its small, little eyes seeming to eat her up. "Take your time! Remember! One more guess, and you're mine!"

Well, she backed off a bit from that Imp, for it was just horrible to look at, but then she laughed and pointed her finger at it and said:

"Name me, name me not,
   Your name is
      Tom
      TIT
      TOT."

And you never heard such a shriek as that small, little Imp gave out. Its tail dropped down straight, its feet all crumpled up, and away it flew into the dark, and she never saw it again.

And she lived happily ever after with her husband, the King.

THE GOLDEN SNUFFBOX

ONCE upon a time, there lived a man and a woman who had one son called Jack, and he was terribly fond of reading books. He read and he read, and then, because his parents lived in a lonely house in a lonely forest and he never saw any other folk but his father and his mother, he became quite crazy to go out into the world and see charming princesses and the like.

So one day he told his mother he must be off, and she called him an air-brained muddlehead, but added that, as he was no use at home, he had better go seek his fortune. Then she asked him if he would rather take a small cake with her blessing to eat on his journey, or a large cake with her curse. Now, Jack was a very hungry lad, so he just up and said, "A big cake, if you please."

So his mother made a great big cake, and when he started off, she went up to the top of the house and cast curses on him, till he was out of sight. You see, she had to do it, but after that she sat down and cried.

Well, Jack hadn't gone far when he came to a field where his father was plowing. Now the good man was dreadfully upset when he found his son was going away, and still more so when he heard he had chosen his mother's curse. So he cast about for what to do to put things straight, and at last he drew out of his pocket a little golden snuffbox, and gave it to the lad, saying, "If ever you are in danger of sudden death, you may open the box, but not till then. It has been in our family for years and years, but, as we have lived, father and son, quietly in the forest, none of us have ever been in need of help—perhaps you may."

So Jack pocketed the golden snuffbox and went on his way.

After a time, he grew very tired, and very hungry, for he had eaten his big cake first thing and night closed in on him so that he could scarcely see his way.

But at last he came to a large house and begged board and lodging at the back door. Jack was a good-looking young fellow, so the servant at once called him in to the fireside and gave him plenty of good meat and bread and beer. And it so happened that while he was eating his supper, the master's lively young daughter came into the kitchen and saw him. She went to her father and said that there was the handsomest young fellow she had ever seen in the back kitchen, and that if her father loved her, he would give the young man some employment. Now the gentleman of the house was exceedingly fond of his bright young daughter, and did not want to vex her, so he went into the back kitchen and questioned Jack as to what he could do.

"Anything," said Jack gaily, meaning, of course, that he could do any sort of work about a house.

But the gentleman saw a way of pleasing his daughter and getting rid of the trouble of employing Jack; so he laughed and said, "If you can do anything, my good lad, you had better do this. By eight o'clock tomorrow morning you must have dug a lake four miles round in front of my mansion, and on it there must be floating a whole fleet of vessels. And they must range up in front of my mansion and fire a salute of guns. And the very last shot must break the leg of the fourposter bed on which my daughter sleeps, for she is always late in the morning!"

Well! Jack was terribly flabbergasted, but he faltered out, "And if I don't do it?"

"Then," said the master of the house quite calmly, "your life will be the forfeit."

So he bade the servants take Jack to a turret room and lock the door on him.

Well! Jack sat on the side of his bed and tried to think things out, but he felt as if he didn't know anything, so he decided to think no more, and after saying his prayers, he lay down and went to sleep. And he did sleep! When he woke it was close to eight o'clock, and he had only time to fly to the window and look out, when the great clock on the tower began to whirr before it struck the hour. And there was the lawn in front of the house all set with beds of roses and marigolds! Then, all of a sudden, he remembered the little golden snuffbox.

"I'm near enough to death," quoth he to himself, as he drew it out and opened it.

And no sooner had he opened it than out hopped three funny little red men in red nightcaps, rubbing their eyes and yawning, for, you see, they had been locked up in the box for years and years and years.

The Golden Snuffbox

"What do you want, Master?" they said between their yawns. But Jack heard that clock a-whirring and knew he hadn't a moment to lose, so he just jabbered off his orders. Then the clock began to strike, and the little men flew out of the window, and suddenly:

Bang! Bang! Bang! Bang! Bang! Bang!

went the guns, and the last one must have broken the leg of the fourposter bed, for there at the window was the bright young daughter in her nightcap, gazing with astonishment at the lake four miles round, with the fleet of vessels floating on it!

And so did Jack! He had never seen such a sight in his life, and he was quite sorry when the three little red men disturbed him by flying in through the window and scrambling into the golden snuffbox.

"Give us a little more time when you want us next, Master," they said sulkily. Then they shut down the lid, and Jack could hear them yawning inside as they settled down to sleep.

As you may imagine, the master of the house was much astonished. As for the lively young daughter, she declared at once that she would never marry anyone else but the young man who could do such wonderful things; the truth was that she and Jack had fallen in love with each other at first sight.

But her father was cautious. "It is true, my dear," said he, "that the young fellow seems a splendid boy; but for all we know it may be chance, not skill, and he may have some fatal flaw. So we must try him again."

Then he said to Jack, "My daughter must have a fine house

to live in. Therefore by tomorrow morning at eight o'clock there must be a magnificent castle standing on twelve golden pillars in the middle of the lake, and there must be a church beside it. And all things must be ready for the bride, and at eight o'clock precisely, a peal of bells from the church must ring out for the wedding. If not, you will have to forfeit your life."

This time Jack intended to give the three little red men more time for their task; but what with having enjoyed himself so much all day, and having eaten so much good food, he overslept, so that the big clock on the tower was whirring before it struck eight when he woke, leapt out of bed, and rushed to the golden snuffbox. But he had forgotten where he had put it, and so the clock had *really* begun to strike before he found it under his pillow, opened it, and jabbered out his orders. And then you never would believe how the three little red men tumbled over each other and yawned and stretched and made haste all at one time, so that Jack thought his life would surely be forfeited. But just as the clock struck its last chime, out rang a peal of merry bells, and there was the castle standing on twelve golden pillars and a church beside it in the middle of the lake. And the castle was all decorated for the wedding, and there were crowds and crowds of servants and retainers, all dressed in their Sunday best.

Never before had Jack seen such a sight; neither had the bright young daughter who, of course, was looking out of the next window in her nightcap. And she looked so pretty and so happy that Jack felt quite cross when he had to step back to let the three little red men fly to their golden snuffbox. But they were far crosser than he was, and mumbled and grumbled at the hustle, so that Jack was quite glad when they shut the box and began to snore.

Well, of course, Jack and the bright young daughter were married, and were as happy as the day is long; and Jack had fine clothes to wear, fine food to eat, fine servants to wait on him, and as many fine friends as he liked.

So he was in luck; but he had yet to learn that a mother's curse is sure to bring misfortune some time or another.

Thus it happened that one day when he was going hunting with all the ladies and gentlemen, Jack forgot to change the golden snuffbox (which he always carried around with him for fear of accidents) from his vest pocket to that of his scarlet hunting coat; so he left it behind. And what should happen but that the servant let it fall on the ground when he was folding up the clothes, and the snuffbox flew open and out popped the three little red men yawning and stretching.

Well! When they found out that they hadn't really been summoned, and that there was no fear of death, they were in a towering temper and said they had a great mind to fly away with the castle, golden pillars and all.

On hearing this, the servant pricked up his ears.

"Could you do that?" he asked.

"Could we?" they said, and they laughed aloud. "Why, we can do anything."

Then the servant said ever so sharply, "Then move this castle and all it contains right away over the sea where the master can't disturb us."

Now the little red men need not really have obeyed the

order, but they were so cross with Jack that hardly had the servant said the words before the task was done. When the hunting party came back, lo and behold! The castle and the church and the golden pillars had all disappeared!

At first, all the others set upon Jack for being a knave and a cheat, and, in particular, his wife's father threatened to punish him for deceiving his daughter. But at last he agreed to let Jack have twelve months and a day to find the castle and bring it back.

So off Jack started on a good horse with some money in his pocket.

And he traveled far and he traveled fast, and he traveled east and west, north and south, over hills and dales, and valleys and mountains, and woods and sheepwalks, but never a sign of the missing castle did he see. Now at last he came to the palace of the King of all the Mice in the Wide World. And there was a little mousie in fine armor and a steel cap doing sentry duty at the front gate, and he was not about to let Jack in until he had told his errand. And when Jack had told it, he passed him on to the next mouse sentry at the inner gate; so by degrees, he reached the King's chamber, where he sat surrounded by mice courtiers.

Now the King of the Mice received Jack very graciously, and said that he himself knew nothing of the missing castle, but, as he was King of all the Mice in the whole world, it was possible that some of his subjects might know more than he. So he ordered his chamberlain to command a Grand Assembly for the next morning, and in the meantime he entertained Jack royally.

The Golden Snuffbox

But the next morning, though there were brown mice and black mice, and gray mice and white mice, and spotted mice, from all parts of the world, they all answered with one breath, "If it please your Majesty, we have not seen the missing castle."

Then the King said, "You must go and ask my elder brother the King of all the Frogs. He may be able to tell you. Leave your horse here and take one of mine. It knows the way and will carry you safely."

So Jack set off on the King's horse, and as he passed the outer gate he saw the little mouse sentry coming away, for its guard duty was over. Now Jack was a kindhearted lad, and he had saved some crumbs from his dinner in order to recompense the little sentry for his kindness. So he put his hand in his pocket and pulled out the crumbs.

"Here you are, little mouse," he said. "That's for your trouble!"

Then the mouse thanked him kindly and asked if he would take him along to the King of the Frogs.

"Not I," said Jack. "I should get into trouble with your King."

But the mousekin insisted. "I may be of some use to you," it said. So it ran up the horse's hind leg and up past its tail and hid in Jack's pocket. And the horse set off at a fast gallop, for it didn't really like the mouse running over it.

At last Jack came to the palace of the King of all the Frogs, and there at the front gate was a frog sentry in a fine coat of mail and a brass helmet. And the frog sentry did not want to let Jack in, but the mouse called out that they came from the King of all the Mice and must be let in without delay. So they were taken to the King's chamber, where he sat surrounded by frog courtiers in fine clothes. But he had heard nothing of the castle on golden pillars, and though he summoned all the frogs of all the world to a Grand Assembly next morning, they all answered his question with, *"Kro kro, Kro kro,"* which everyone knows stands for "No" in frog language.

So the King said to Jack, "There remains but one thing. You must go and ask my eldest brother, the King of all the Birds. His subjects are always on the wing, so perhaps they have seen something. Leave the horse you are riding here, and take one of mine. It knows the way, and will carry you safely."

So Jack set off, and being a kindhearted lad he gave the frog sentry, whom he met coming away from guard duty, some crumbs he had saved from his dinner. And the frog asked leave to go with him, and when Jack refused to take him he just gave one hop on to the stirrup, and a second hop on to the rear, and in the next hop, he was in Jack's other pocket.

Then the horse galloped away like lightning, for it didn't like the slimy frog coming down *"plop!"* on its back.

Well, after a time, Jack came to the palace of the King of all the Birds, and there at the front gate were a sparrow and a crow marching up and down with guns on their shoulders. Now at this Jack laughed very hard, and the mouse and the frog called out from his pockets, "We come from the King! Let us pass."

The sentries were amazed, and let them pass without more ado.

But when they came to the King's chamber, where he sat surrounded by all manner of birds—tomtits, wrens, cormorants, turtledoves, and the like—the King said he was sorry, but he had no news of the missing castle. And though he summoned all the birds of all the world to a Grand Assembly next morning, not one of them had seen or heard tell of it.

So Jack was quite disconsolate till the King said, "But where is the eagle? I don't see my eagle."

Then the Chamberlain—he was a tomtit—stepped forward with a bow and said, "May it please your Majesty he is late."

"Late?" said the King, fuming. "Summon him at once."

So two larks flew up into the sky till they couldn't be seen and sang ever so loud, till at last the eagle appeared all in a sweat from having flown so fast.

Then the King said, "Sir! Have you seen a missing castle that stands upon twelve pillars of gold?"

And the eagle blinked its eyes and said, "May it please your Majesty, that is where I've been."

Then everybody rejoiced exceedingly, and when the eagle had eaten and rested so as to be strong enough for the journey, he spread his wide wings, on which Jack stood, with the mouse in one pocket and the frog in the other, and started off in obedience to the King's order to take the owner back to his missing castle as quickly as possible.

And they flew over land and they flew over sea, until at last in the far distance they saw the castle standing on its twelve golden pillars. But all the doors and windows were shut fast and barred, for, you see, the servant who had run away with it had gone out hunting for the day, and he always bolted the doors and windows of the castle while he was absent lest someone else should run away with it.

So Jack was puzzled as to how he could get hold of the

golden snuffbox, until the little mouse said, "Let me fetch it. There is always a mouse hole in every castle, so I am sure I shall be able to get in."

So off it went, and Jack waited on the eagle's wings in agony, till at last the mousekin appeared.

"Have you got it?" shouted Jack, and the little mousie cried, "Yes!"

So everyone rejoiced mightily, and they set off back to the palace of the King of all the Birds, where Jack had left his horse, for now that he had the golden snuffbox safe, he knew he could get the castle back whenever he chose to send the three little red men to fetch it. But on the way over the sea, while Jack, who was dead tired with standing so long, lay down between the eagle's wings and fell asleep, the mouse and the eagle fell to quarreling as to which of them had helped Jack the most, and they quarreled so much that at last they laid the case before the frog. Then the frog, who made a very wise judge, said he must see the whole affair from the very beginning. So the mouse brought out the golden snuffbox from Jack's pocket, and began to relate where it had been found and all about it. Now, at that very moment Jack awoke, kicked out his leg, and plump went the golden snuffbox down to the very bottom of the sea!

"I thought my turn would come," said the frog, and went *"plump!"* in after it.

Well, they waited and waited and waited for three whole days and three whole nights; but froggie never came up again, and they had just given him up in despair when his nose showed above the water.

"Have you got it?" they shouted.

"No!" said he, with a great gasp.

"Then what do you want?" they cried, in a rage.

"My breath," said froggie, and with that he sank down again.

Well, they waited two days and two nights more, and at last up came the little frog with the golden snuffbox in its mouth.

Then they all rejoiced mightily, and the eagle flew ever so fast to the palace of the King of the Birds.

But alas, and alack-a-day—Jack's troubles were not ended; his mother's curse was still bringing him ill luck, for the King of the Birds flew into a fearsome rage because Jack had not brought the castle of the golden pillars back with him. And he said that unless he saw it by eight o'clock next morning Jack's head should come off for being a cheat and a liar.

Then Jack, being close to death, opened the golden snuffbox, and out tumbled the three little red men in their three little red caps. They had recovered their tempers and were quite glad to be back with a master who knew that they would only, as a rule, work under fear of death; for, you see, the servant had been forever disturbing their sleep with opening the box for no reason.

So before the clock struck eight next morning, there was the castle on its twelve golden pillars, and the King of the Birds was pleased, and let Jack take his horse and ride to the palace of the King of the Frogs. But there, exactly the same thing happened, and poor Jack had to open the snuffbox again and order the castle to come to the palace of the King of the Frogs.

The Golden Snuffbox

At this, the little red men were a wee bit cross; but they said they supposed it could not be helped. So though they yawned, they brought the castle all right, and Jack was allowed to take his horse and go to the palace of the King of all the Mice in the World. But here the same thing happened, and the little red men tumbled out of the golden snuffbox in a real rage, and said fellows might as well have no sleep at all! However, they did as they were bidden: they brought the castle of the golden pillars from the palace of the King of the Frogs to the palace of the King of the Mice, and Jack was allowed to take his own horse and ride home.

But the year and a day which he had been allowed was almost gone, and even his lively young wife, after almost weeping her eyes out over her handsome young husband, had given up Jack for lost; so everyone was astounded to see him, and not

31

overly pleased either to see him come without his castle. In-deed, his father-in-law swore with many oaths that if it were not in its proper place by eight o'clock next morning, Jack's life should be forfeited.

Now this, of course, was exactly what Jack had wanted and intended from the beginning; because when death was near, he could open the golden snuffbox and order the little red men about. But he had opened it so often of late, and they had become so cross, that he was in a stew what to do; whether to give them time to show their temper, or to hustle them out of it. At last he decided to do half of one and half of the other. So just as the hands of the clock were at five minutes to eight, he opened the box, and stopped his ears!

Well! You never heard such a yawning, and scolding, and threatening, and blustering! What did he mean by it? Why should he take four bites at one cherry? If he was always in fear of death, why didn't he die and have done with it?

In the midst of all this the tower clock began to whirr—

"Gentlemen!" said Jack—he was really quaking with fear—"Do as you are told."

"For the last time," they shrieked. "We won't stay and serve a master who thinks he is going to die every day."

And with that they flew out of the window.

AND THEY NEVER CAME BACK.

The golden snuffbox remained empty forever.

But when Jack looked out of window, there was the castle

in the middle of the lake on its twelve golden pillars, and there
was his young wife ever so pretty in her nightcap, looking out
of the window.

And they lived happily ever after.

TATTERCOATS

IN a great palace by the sea there once dwelt a very rich old lord, who had neither wife nor children living, only one little granddaughter, whose face he had never seen in all her life. He hated her bitterly, because at her birth his favorite daughter died, and when the old nurse brought him the baby he swore that he would never look on its face as long as it lived.

So he turned his back, and sat by his window looking out over the sea, and weeping great tears for his lost daughter, till his white hair and beard grew down over his shoulders and twined round his chair and crept into the chinks of the floor, and his tears, dropping on to the window ledge, wore a channel through the stone, and ran away in a little river to the great sea.

Meanwhile, his granddaughter grew up with no one to care for her, or clothe her. When no one was around, the old nurse would sometimes give her a dish of scraps from the kitchen, or a torn petticoat from the rag bag, but the other servants of the palace would drive her from the house with mocking words, calling her "Tattercoats," and pointing to her bare feet and shoulders, till she ran away, crying, to hide among the bushes.

So she grew up, with little to eat or to wear, spending her

days out of doors, her only companion a crippled gooseherd, who fed his flock of geese on the common. And this gooseherd was an odd, merry little chap, and when she was hungry, or cold, or tired, he would play to her gaily on his little pipe, until she forgot all her troubles, and began to dance with his flock of noisy geese for partners.

Now one day word spread that the King was traveling through the land, and was to give a great ball for all the lords and ladies of the country in the town nearby, and that the Prince, his only son, was to choose a wife from among the maidens. In due time a royal invitation to the ball was brought to the palace by the sea, and the servants carried it up to the old lord, who still sat by his window, wrapped in his long white hair and weeping into the little river that was fed by his tears.

But when he heard the King's command, he dried his eyes and told them to bring shears to cut him loose, for his hair had bound him fast, and he could not move. And then he sent them for rich clothes and jewels, which he put on; and he ordered them to saddle the white horse, with gold and silk, that he might ride to meet the King. But he quite forgot he had a granddaughter to take to the ball.

Meanwhile, Tattercoats sat by the kitchen door weeping, because she could not go to see the grand doings. And when the old nurse heard her crying she went to the lord of the palace, and begged him to take his granddaughter with him to the King's ball.

But he only frowned and told her to be silent, while the

servants laughed and said, "Tattercoats is happy in her rags, playing with the gooseherd! Let her be—it is all she is fit for."

A second, and then a third time, the old nurse begged him to let the girl go with him, but she was answered by black looks and fierce words, till she was driven from the room by the jeering servants, with blows and mocking words.

Weeping, the old nurse went to look for Tattercoats, but the girl had been turned from the door by the cook, and had run away to tell her friend the gooseherd how unhappy she was because she could not go to the King's ball.

Now when the gooseherd had listened to her story, he told her to cheer up, and proposed that they should go together into the town to see the King and all the fine things; and when she looked sorrowfully down at her rags and bare feet he played a note or two upon his pipe, so gay and merry, that she forgot all about her tears and her troubles, and before she knew it, the gooseherd had taken her by the hand, and, together, with the geese before them, they went dancing down the road towards the town.

Before they had gone very far, a handsome young man, splendidly dressed, rode up and stopped to ask the way to the castle where the King was staying. When he learned that they too were going there, he got off his horse and walked beside them along the road.

"You seem merry folk," he said, "and will be good company."

"Good company, indeed," said the gooseherd, and played a new tune that was not a dance.

It was a curious tune, and it made the fine young man stare

and stare and stare at Tattercoats till he couldn't see her rags—till he couldn't, to tell the truth, see anything but her beautiful face.

Then he said, "You are the most beautiful maiden in the world. Will you marry me?"

Then the gooseherd smiled to himself, and played sweeter than ever.

But Tattercoats laughed. "Not I," said she. "You would be put to shame, and so would I, if you took a goosegirl for your wife! Go and ask one of the great ladies you will see tonight at the King's ball, and do not tease poor Tattercoats."

But the more she refused him the sweeter the pipe played, and the deeper the young man fell in love; till at last he begged her to come that night at midnight to the King's ball, just as she was, with the gooseherd and his geese, in her torn petticoat and bare feet, and see if he wouldn't dance with her before the King and the lords and ladies, and present her to them all, as his dear and honored bride.

Now at first Tattercoats refused; but the gooseherd said, "Take fortune when it comes, little one."

So night came, and the hall in the castle was full of light and music, and the lords and ladies were dancing before the King. Just as the clock struck twelve, Tattercoats and the gooseherd, followed by his flock of noisy geese, hissing and swaying their heads, entered at the great doors, and walked straight up the ballroom, while on either side the ladies whispered, the lords laughed, and the King seated at the far end stared in amazement.

But as they came before the throne the handsome young

man rose from beside the King, and came to meet her. Taking her by the hand, he kissed her thrice before them all, and turned to the King.

"Father!" he said—for it was the Prince himself—"I have made my choice, and here is my bride, the loveliest girl in all the land, and the sweetest as well!"

Before he had finished speaking, the gooseherd had put his pipe to his lips and played a few notes that sounded like a bird singing far off in the woods. And as he played Tattercoats' rags were changed to shining robes sewn with glittering jewels, a golden crown lay upon her golden hair, and the flock of geese behind her became a crowd of dainty pages, bearing her long train.

And as the King rose to greet her as his daughter-in-law the trumpets sounded loudly in honor of the new Princess, and the people outside in the street said to each other, "Ah! The Prince has chosen for his wife the loveliest girl in all the land!"

But the gooseherd was never seen again, and no one knew what became of him; while the old lord went home once more to his palace by the sea, for he could not stay at court when he had sworn never to look on his granddaughter's face.

So there he still sits by his window—if you could only see him, as you may some day—weeping more bitterly than ever. And his white hair has bound him once more to the stones, and the river of his tears runs away to the great sea.

THE THREE FEATHERS

ONCE upon a time there lived a girl who was wooed by, and later married to, a man she never saw; for he came courting her after nightfall, and when they were married he never came home till it was dark, and always left before dawn.

Still he was good and kind to her, giving her everything her heart could desire, so she was well content for a while. But, after a bit, some of her friends, full of envy for her good luck, began to whisper that her unseen husband must have something dreadful the matter with him which made him shy away from being seen.

Now from the very beginning, the girl had wondered why her lover did not come courting her as other girls' lovers came, openly and by day. Although, at first, she paid no heed to her neighbors' nods and winks, she began at last to think there might be something in what they said. So she decided to see for herself, and one night when she heard her husband come into her room, she lit her candle suddenly and saw him.

And, lo and behold! He was handsome as handsome could be; handsome enough to make every woman in the world fall in love with him on the spot. But even as she got a glimpse of him, he changed into a big brown bird which looked at her with eyes full of anger and blame.

The Three Feathers

"Because you have done this thing," it said, "you will see me no more, unless for seven long years and a day you serve me faithfully."

And she cried with tears and sobs, "I will serve seven times seven years and a day if only you will come back. Tell me what I am to do."

Then the bird-husband said, "I will place you in service, and there you must remain and do good work for seven years and a day, and you must listen to no man who tempts you to leave that service. If you do I will never return."

To this the girl agreed, and the bird, spreading its broad brown wings, carried her to a big mansion.

"Here they need a laundrymaid," said the bird-husband. "Go in, ask to see the mistress, and say you will do the work—but remember you must do it for seven years and a day."

"But I cannot do it for even seven days," answered the girl. "I cannot wash or iron."

"That matters nothing," replied the bird. "All you have to do is to pluck three feathers from under my wing close to my heart, and these feathers will do your bidding whatever it may be. You will only have to put them on your hand, and say, 'By virtue of these three feathers from over my true love's heart may this be done,' and it will be done."

So the girl plucked three feathers from under the bird's wing, and after that the bird flew away.

Then the girl did as she was bidden, and the lady of the house engaged her for the place. And never did you see such a quick laundress; for, you see, she had only to go into the washhouse, bolt the door and close the shutters, so no one could see her. Then she would pull out the three feathers and say, "By virtue of these three feathers from over my true love's heart may the fire be lit, the clothes sorted, washed, boiled, dried, folded, and ironed," and lo! The clothes came tumbling onto the table, clean and white, ready to be put away. Her mistress set great store by her and said there never was such a good laundry maid. Thus passed four years and there was no talk of her leaving. But the other servants grew jealous of her, all the more so, because, being a very pretty girl, all the men-servants fell in love with her and wanted to marry her.

But she would have none of them, because she was always waiting and longing for the day when her bird-husband would come back to her in man's form.

Now one of the men who wanted her was the stout butler, and one day as he was coming back from the ciderhouse he chanced to stop by the laundry, and he heard a voice say, "By virtue of these three feathers from over my true love's heart may the fire be lit, the clothes sorted, boiled, dried, folded, and ironed."

He thought this very odd, so he peeped through the key-hole. And there was the girl sitting at her ease in a chair, while all the clothes came flying to the table ready to put away.

Well, that night he went to the girl and said that if she turned up her nose at him and his proposal any longer, he would tell the mistress that her fine laundress was nothing but a witch; and then, even if she were not burnt at the stake, she would at least lose her job.

Now the girl was in great distress, since if she failed to serve her seven years and a day in one service, her bird-husband would fail to return. So she made an excuse by saying she could think of no one who could give her enough money to satisfy her.

At this the stout butler laughed. "Money?" said he. "I have seventy pounds laid by with the master. Won't that satisfy you?"

"It would," she replied.

So the very next night the butler came to her with the seventy pounds in golden sovereigns, and she held out her apron and took them, saying she was content—for she had thought of a plan.

As they were going upstairs together she stopped and said, "Mr. Butler, excuse me for a minute. I have left the shutters of the washhouse open, and I must shut them, or they will be banging all night and disturb master and missus!"

Now though the butler was stout and beginning to grow old, he was anxious to seem young and gallant; so he said at once, "Excuse me, my beauty, you shall not go. I will go myself and shut them. I won't be but a moment!"

So off he set, and no sooner had he gone than she pulled out her three feathers, and putting them on her hand, said in a hurry, "By virtue of the three feathers from over my true love's heart may the shutters never cease banging till morning, and may Mr. Butler's hands be busy trying to shut them."

And so it happened. Mr. Butler shut the shutters, but—bru-u-u! There they were hanging open again. Then he shut them once more, and this time they hit him on the face as they flew open. Yet he couldn't stop trying; he had to go on. So there he was the whole night long. Such banging, and swearing, and shutting there never was, until dawn came and, too tired to be really angry, he crept back to his bed, resolving that come what might he would not tell what had happened to him or else he would be a laughingstock. So he kept quiet, and the girl kept the seventy pounds, and laughed up her sleeve.

After a time the coachman, a neat middle-aged man, who had long wanted to marry the pretty laundrymaid, on his way to the pump to get water for his horses, overheard her giving orders to the three feathers. Peeping through the keyhole as the butler had done, he saw her sitting at her ease in a chair while the clothes, all washed and ironed and folded, came flying to the table.

Just as the butler had done, he went to the girl and said, "I have you now, my pretty. Don't dare to turn up your nose at me, for if you do I'll tell mistress you are a witch."

Then the girl said quite calmly, "I look on none who has no money."

"If that is all," replied the coachman, "I have forty pounds saved up. I'll bring it tomorrow night."

So when the night came the girl held out her apron for the money, and as she was going up the stairs she stopped suddenly and said, "Goodness! I've left my clothes on the line. Wait till I fetch them in."

Now the coachman was really a very polite fellow, so he said at once, "Let me go. It is a cold, windy night and you'll be catching your death."

So off he went, and the girl took out her feathers and said, "By virtue of the three feathers from over my true love's heart may the clothes slash and blow about till dawn, and may Mr.

Coachman not be able to gather them up or take his hand from the job.''

And when she had said this she went quietly to bed, for she knew what would happen. And sure enough it did. There never was such a night as Mr. Coachman spent with the wet clothes flittering and fluttering about his ears, and the sheets wrapping him into a bundle, and tripping him up, while the towels slashed at his legs. But though he smarted all over he had to go on till dawn came, and then the very weary, woebegone coachman couldn't even creep away to his bed, for he had to feed and water his horses! And he, also, kept his own counsel for fear that his friends would laugh at him. So the clever laundrymaid put the forty pounds with the seventy in her box, and gaily went on with her work.

Then after a time the footman, who was quite an honest lad and truly in love, was going by the laundry. He peeped through the keyhole to get a glimpse of his dearest dear, and what should he see but her sitting at her ease in a chair, and the clothes coming all ready folded and ironed onto the table.

Now when he saw this he was greatly troubled. So he went to his master and drew out all his savings, and then he went to the girl and told her that he would have to tell the mistress what he had seen, unless she consented to marry him.

''You see,'' he said, ''I have worked here a long while and have saved up this bit, and you also have been here a long while and must have saved as well. So let us put our savings together and make a home, or else stay here, as you please.''

Well, she tried to put him off; but he insisted so much that at last she said, "James! There's a dear, run down to the cellar and fetch me a drop of brandy. You've made me feel so odd!"

And when he had gone she took out her three feathers, and said, "By virtue of the three feathers from over my true love's heart may James not be able to pour the brandy straight, except down his throat."

Well! So it happened. Try as he would, James could not get the brandy into the glass. A few drops splashed into it, then trickled over his hand, and fell on the floor. And so it went on and on till he grew so tired that he thought he needed a drink himself. So he tossed off a few drops and began again, but he fared no better. So he took another little drop, and went on, and on, and on, till he got quite befuddled. And who should come down into the cellar but his master to know what the smell of brandy meant!

Now James the footman was truthful as well as honest, so he told the master how he had come down to get the sick laundrymaid a drop of brandy, but that his hand had shaken so that he could not pour it out, and it had fallen on the ground, and that the smell of it had got to his head.

"A likely tale," said the master, and chastised James soundly.

Then the master went to the mistress, his wife, and said, "Send away that laundrymaid of yours. Something has come over my men. They have all drawn out their savings as if they were going to be married, yet they don't leave, and I believe that girl is at the bottom of it."

But his wife would not hear of the laundrymaid being blamed; she was the best servant in the house, and worth all the

rest of them put together; it was his men who were at fault. So
they quarreled over it; but in the end the master gave in, and
after this there was peace, since the mistress told the girl to
keep herself to herself, and none of the men would tell what
had happened for fear of the laughter of the other servants.

So it went on until one day when the master was going for
a drive, the coach was at the door, and the footman was standing to hold the coach open, and the butler on the steps all
ready, when who should pass through the yard, so saucy and
bright with a great basket of clean clothes, but the laundrymaid. And the sight of her was too much for James, the
footman, who began to blub.

"She is a wicked girl," he said. "She got all my savings, and
got me a good thrashing besides."

Then the coachman grew bold. "Did she?" he said. "That
is nothing to what she did to me." So he told all about the wet
clothes and the awful job he had had the whole night long.
Now the butler on the steps swelled with rage until he nearly
burst, and at last he came out with his night of banging
shutters.

"And one," he said, "hit me on the nose."

This united the three men, and they agreed to tell their
master the moment he came out, and get the girl sent away.
Now the laundrymaid had sharp ears and had paused behind a
door to listen; when she heard this she knew she must do
something to stop it. So she took out her three feathers and
said, "By virtue of the three feathers from over my true love's
heart may there be arguing as to who suffered most between
the men until they all fall into the pond for a ducking."

Tattercoats dancing while the gooseherd pipes

Page 37

The giant Cormoran was the terror of all the countryside
Page 51

The Three Feathers

Well! No sooner had she said the words than the three men began fighting over which of them had suffered most. James up and hit the stout butler, giving him a black eye, and the fat butler fell upon James and pommeled him hard, while the coachman scrambled from his box and knocked them both about, and the laundrymaid stood by laughing.

Out came the master, but none of them would listen, and each wanted to be heard, and fought, and shoved, and pommeled away until they shoved each other into the pond, and all got a fine ducking.

Then the master asked the girl what it was all about, and she said, "They all wanted to tell a story against me because I won't marry them, and one said his was the best, and the next said his was the best, so they fell to quarreling as to which was the likeliest story to get me into trouble. But they are well punished, so there is no need to do more."

Then the master went to his wife and said, "You are right. That laundrymaid of yours is a very wise girl."

So the butler and the coachman and James could only look sheepish and hold their tongues, and the laundrymaid went on with her duties without further trouble.

When the seven years and a day were over, who should drive up to the door in a fine gilded coach but the bird-husband restored to his shape as a handsome young man. And he carried the laundrymaid off to be his wife again, and her master and mistress were so pleased at her good fortune that they ordered all the other servants to stand on the steps and wish her good luck. As she passed the butler she put a bag with seventy pounds in it into his hand and said sweetly, "That is to recompense you for shutting the shutters."

And when she passed the coachman she put a bag with forty pounds into his hand and said, "That is your reward for bringing in the clothes." But when she passed the footman she gave him a bag with a hundred pounds in it, and laughed, saying, "That is for the drop of brandy you never brought me!"

So she drove off with her handsome husband, and lived happily ever after.

JACK THE GIANT-KILLER

I

WHEN good King Arthur reigned with Guinevere, his Queen, there lived in Cornwall, in the south of England, a farmer who had one only son named Jack. Jack was strong and bright, with such a lively mind that no one could best him.

In those days, the Mount of St. Michael isle in Cornwall was the retreat of a huge giant whose name was Cormoran.

He was eighteen feet tall, some three yards around his middle, with a grim, fierce face, and he was the terror of the entire countryside. He lived in a cave within the rocky Mount, and when he needed food he would wade across the tides to the mainland and help himself to all that he came across. Poor folk and rich folk alike ran out of their houses and hid themselves when they heard the swish-swash of his big feet in the water, for if he were to see them, they would lose their lives. As it was, he seized their cattle by the dozen, carrying off several fat oxen on his back at a time, and hanging sheep and pigs from his belt like bunches of keys. Now this had gone on for many years, and the poor folk of Cornwall were in despair, for none could put an end to the giant Cormoran.

It so happened that one market day, Jack, then quite a

young lad, found the town in turmoil over some new exploit of the giant's. Women were weeping, men were cursing, and the magistrates were sitting in council over what was to be done. But none could suggest a plan. Then Jack, blithe as you please, went up to the magistrates, and with fine courtesy—for he was always polite—asked them what reward would be given for the killing of the giant, Cormoran.

"The treasures of the giant's cave," said they.

"Every bit of it?" asked Jack, who was never to be short-changed.

"To the last coin," said they.

"Then I will take the job," said Jack, and forthwith set about the business.

It was wintertime, and having got himself a horn, a pick-axe, and a shovel, he went over to the Mount in the dark of night and set to work, and before dawn, he had dug a pit no less than twenty-two feet deep and nearly as big across. This he covered with long thin sticks and straw, sprinkling a little loose mud over all to make it look like solid ground. And just as dawn was breaking, he planted himself squarely on the side of the pit that was farthest from the giant's cave, raised the horn to his lips, and with a full blast, blew, "Tantivy! Tantivy! Tantivy!" just as he would have done had he been hunting a fox.

Of course this woke the giant, who rushed in a rage out of his cave, and seeing little Jack blowing away at his horn, as calm and cool as could be, he became still more angry, and went after the disturber of his rest, bawling out, "I'll teach you to wake a giant, you little whippersnapper. You shall pay dearly for your tantivys. I'll take you and broil you whole for break——"

He had only got as far as this when crash—he fell into the pit! That was a crash indeed, such a one that it caused the very foundations of the Mount to shake.

Jack shook with laughter. "Ho, ho!" he cried. "How about breakfast now, Sir Giant? Will you have me broiled or baked? And will you serve nothing but poor little Jack? Faith! You're in the stocks for bad behavior, and I'll punish you as I like. I wish I had rotten eggs, but this will do as well." And with that, he lifted his pickaxe and dealt Cormoran such a mighty blow on the top of his head that he killed him on the spot.

Whereupon Jack calmly filled up the pit with earth and went to search the cave, where he found a great deal of treasure.

When the magistrates heard of Jack's great exploit, they proclaimed that henceforth he should be known as Jack the Giant-Killer. And they presented him with a sword and belt, on which these words were embroidered in gold:

Here's the valiant Cornishman
Who slew the giant Cormoran.

II

Of course the news of Jack's victory soon spread over all of England, so that another giant named Blunderbore, who lived to the north, hearing of it, vowed if ever he came across Jack, he would take revenge upon him. Now this giant Blunderbore was lord of an enchanted castle that stood in the middle of a lonely forest.

It so happened that about four months after he had killed Cormoran, Jack had occasion to journey into Wales, and on the road, he passed this forest. Weary with walking, and finding a pleasant fountain by the wayside, he lay down to rest and was soon fast asleep.

The giant Blunderbore, coming to the well for water, found Jack sleeping, and knew by the lines embroidered on his belt that he was the far-famed giant-killer. Rejoicing at his luck, the giant, immediately lifted Jack to his shoulder and began to carry him through the wood to the enchanted castle.

But the rustling of the boughs awakened Jack, who, finding himself already in the clutches of the giant, was terrified; nor was his alarm decreased by seeing the courtyard of the castle strewn with men's bones.

"Yours will be with them before long," said Blunderbore, as he locked poor Jack in an immense chamber above the castle gateway. It had a high-pitched, beamed roof, and one window that looked down the road. Here poor Jack was to stay while Blunderbore went to fetch his brother giant, who lived in the same wood, so he could share in the feast.

After a time, Jack, watching through the window, saw the two giants tramping hastily down the road, eager for their dinner.

"Now," said Jack to himself, "my death or my deliverance is at hand." For he had thought of a plan. In one corner of the room he had seen two strong cords. These he took, and cleverly making a noose with a slipknot at the end of each, he hung them out of the window, and, as the giants were unlocking the iron door of the gate, managed to slip them over their heads without their noticing. Then, quick as a wink, he tied the other ends to a beam, and pulled with all his might, so that the nooses tightened and throttled the giants until they stopped struggling. Seeing this, Jack slid down the ropes, and, drawing his sword, slew them both.

Taking the keys to the castle, he unlocked all the doors and set free three beautiful women who he found tied by the hair of their heads.

"Sweet ladies," said Jack, kneeling on one knee—for he was always polite—"here are the keys to this enchanted castle. I have destroyed the giant Blunderbore and his brutish brother, and thus have restored to you your liberty. These keys should bring you all else you require."

So saying, he proceeded on his journey to Wales.

III

He traveled as fast as he could; perhaps too fast, for, losing his way, he found himself in darkness and far from any habitation. He wandered on hopefully, until, on entering a narrow valley he came on a very large, dreary-looking house standing alone. Being anxious for shelter, he went up to the door and knocked. You may imagine his surprise and alarm when the summons was answered by a giant with two heads. But though this monster's look was exceedingly fierce, his manners were quite polite.

So he welcomed Jack heartily, and prepared a bedroom for him, where he was left with kind wishes for a good rest. Jack, however, was too tired to sleep well, and as he lay awake, he overheard his host muttering to himself in the next room. Having very keen ears, he was able to make out these words, or something like them:

"Though here you lodge with me this night,
You shall not see the morning light.
My club shall dash your brains outright."

"So say you!" said Jack to himself, getting up at once. "So that is your trick, is it? But I will get even with you." Then, leaving his bed, he laid a big wood log under the blankets, and, taking one of these to keep himself warm, made himself snug in a corner of the room, pretending to snore, so as to make Mr. Giant think he was asleep.

And sure enough, after a little time, in came the monster on tiptoe as if treading on eggs, and carrying a big club. Then —WHACK! WHACK! WHACK!

Jack could hear the bed being showered with blows until the Giant, thinking every bone in his guest's body must be broken, stole out of the room again; whereupon Jack went calmly to bed once more and slept soundly! Next morning the giant couldn't believe his eyes when he saw Jack coming down the stairs, fresh and hearty.

"Odds splutter my nails!" he cried, astonished. "Did you sleep well? Was there not nothing felt in the night?"

"Oh," replied Jack, laughing up his sleeve, "I think a rat did come and give me two or three slaps with his tail."

At this, the giant was dumbfounded, and led Jack to breakfast, bringing him a bowl which held at least four gallons of porridge, and bidding him, as a man of such strength, to eat the lot. Now Jack, when traveling, wore under his cloak a leather bag to carry his things. Quick as a wink, he hitched the bag around so the opening was just under his chin; thus, as he ate, he could slip most of the porridge into it without the giant's being any the wiser. So they sat down to breakfast, the giant gobbling down his own measure of porridge, while Jack made away with his.

"See," said crafty Jack when he had finished, "I'll show you a trick worth two of yours." He picked up a carving knife, stuck it into his shirt, and ripped up the leather bag. Out spilled all the porridge onto the floor!

"Odds splutter my nails!" cried the giant, not to be outdone. "I can do that myself!" Whereupon he seized the carving knife, ripped open his own belly, and fell down dead.

Thus was Jack free of that giant.

IV

It so happened that in those days, when gallant knights were always seeking adventures, King Arthur's only son, a very valiant prince, begged his father for a large sum of money so that he could travel to Wales to set free a certain beautiful lady who was possessed by seven evil spirits. In vain the king denied him, and at last he gave in. The prince set out with two horses, one of which he rode, the other laden with gold coins. After some days' journey, the prince came to a market town in Wales where there was a great commotion. On asking the reason, he was told that, according to law, the corpse of a very generous man had been arrested on its way to the grave, because, in life, the man had many unpaid debts.

"That is a cruel law," said the young prince. "Go, bury the dead in peace, and let the creditors come to my lodgings. I will pay the debts of the dead."

So the creditors came, but they were so numerous that by evening the prince had but two pence left for himself, and could not go further on his journey.

It so happened that Jack the Giant-Killer passed through the town on his way to Wales and, hearing of the prince's plight, was so taken with his kindness and generosity that he determined to be the prince's servant. So this was agreed upon, and next morning, after Jack had paid the bill with his last coin, the two set out together. But as they were leaving the town, an old woman ran after the prince and called out, "Justice! Justice! The dead man owed me two pence these seven years. Pay me as well as the others."

And the prince, kind and generous, put his hand into his pocket and gave the old woman the two pence that was left to him. So now they had not a penny between them, and when the sun grew low, the prince said, "Jack! Since we have no money, how are we to get a night's lodging?"

Then Jack replied, "We shall do well enough, Master, for within two or three miles of this place there lives a huge and monstrous giant with three heads, who can fight four hundred men in armor and make them fly from him like chaff before the wind."

"And what good will that be to us?" asked the prince. "He will surely chop us up for a mouthful."

"Nay," said Jack, laughing. "Let me go and prepare the way for you. By all accounts, this giant is a dolt. Perhaps I may manage better than that."

So the prince remained where he was, and Jack pushed his horse to full speed till he came to the giant's castle. He knocked so loud at the gate that he made the neighboring hills resound.

At this, the giant roared from within in a voice like thunder, "Who's there?"

Then said Jack, as bold as brass, "None but your poor cousin Jack."

"Cousin Jack!" said the giant, astounded. "And what news, my poor cousin Jack?" For, you see, he was quite taken aback, so Jack made haste to reassure him.

"Dear coz, heavy news, I fear!"

"Heavy news," echoed the giant, half afraid. "How can heavy news come to me? Have I not three heads? Can I not fight five hundred men in armor? Can I not make them fly like chaff before the wind?"

"True," replied crafty Jack, "but I came to warn you that great King Arthur's son with a thousand men in armor is on his way to kill you." At this, the giant began to shiver and

shake. "Ah! Cousin Jack! Kind cousin Jack! This is heavy news indeed," said he. "Tell me, what am I to do?"

"Hide yourself in the vault," said crafty Jack, "and I will lock and bolt and bar you in, and keep the key till the prince has gone. So you will be safe."

Then the giant hastily ran down into the vault, and Jack locked, bolted, and barred him in. Then being thus secure, he went and fetched his master, and the two made themselves heartily merry over what the giant was to have had for supper, while the miserable monster shivered and shook with fright in the underground vault.

After a good night's rest, Jack woke his master in the early morning, and having furnished him well with gold and silver from the giant's treasure, told him to ride three miles ahead on his journey. And when Jack judged that the prince was pretty well out of range of the smell of the giant, he took the key and let his prisoner out. He was half dead with cold and damp, but very grateful, and he begged Jack to let him know what he could be given as a reward for saving the giant's life and castle from destruction, and he should have it.

"You're very welcome," said Jack, who always had a sharp eye. "All I want is the old coat and cap, together with the rusty old sword and slippers which are at your bedside."

When the giant heard this, he sighed and shook his head. "You don't know what you are asking," he said. "They are the most precious things I possess, but as I have promised, you shall have them. The coat will make you invisible, the cap will tell you all you want to know, the sword will cut to pieces whatever you strike, and the slippers will take you wherever you want to go in the twinkling of an eye!"

Overjoyed, Jack rode away with the coat and cap, the sword and the slippers, and soon overtook his master. They rode on together until they reached the castle where lived the beautiful lady whom the prince sought.

She was very beautiful, although she was possessed by seven evil spirits, and when she heard the prince sought her as a suitor, she smiled and ordered a splendid banquet to be prepared for his reception. And she sat on his right hand, and plied him with food and drink.

And when the repast was over, she took out her own handkerchief and wiped his lips gently, and said, with a smile, "I have a task for you, my lord! You must show me this kerchief tomorrow morning or lose your head."

And with that, she put the handkerchief in her gown and said, "Good night!"

The prince was in despair, but Jack said nothing till his master was in bed. Then he put on the old cap he had gotten from the giant, and lo! In a minute he knew all that he wanted to know. In the dead of the night, when the beautiful lady called on one of her familiar spirits to carry her to the Devil himself, Jack put on his coat of darkness and his slippers of swiftness, and was there as soon as she was. And when she gave the handkerchief to the Devil, bidding him keep it safe, and he put it away on a high shelf, Jack just up and stole it away in a trice!

The next morning, when the enchanted lady expected to see the crestfallen prince, he simply made a fine bow and presented her with the handkerchief.

At first she was terribly disappointed, but, as the day wore on, she ordered another and still more splendid feast. And this time, when the repast was over, she kissed the prince full on the lips and said, "I have a task for you, my suitor. Show me tomorrow morning the last lips I kiss tonight or you lose your head."

Then the prince, who by this time was head over heels in love, said tenderly, "If you will kiss none but mine, I will."

Now the beautiful lady, even though she was possessed by seven evil spirits, could not help seeing that the prince was a very handsome young man, so she blushed a little, and said, "That is neither here nor there. You must show me them, or death is your fate."

So the prince went to his bed, sorrowful as before. But Jack put on the cap of knowledge and knew in a moment all he wanted to know.

Thus when, in the dead of the night, the beautiful lady called on her familiar spirits to take her to the Devil, Jack, in his coat of darkness and his shoes of swiftness, was there before her.

"Thou hast betrayed me once," said the beautiful lady to the Devil, frowning, "by letting go of my handkerchief. Now will I give thee something none can steal, and so defeat the prince, king's son though he be."

With that, she kissed the loathesome demon full on the lips, and left him. Whereupon, Jack with one blow of the rusty sword of strength cut off the Devil's head, and, hiding it under his coat of darkness, brought it back to his master.

The next morning when the lady, with malice in her beautiful eyes, asked the prince to show her the lips she had last kissed, he pulled out the demon's head by the horns. At that, the seven spirits which possessed the poor lady, gave seven dreadful shrieks and left her. Thus the enchantment was broken, and she appeared in all her perfect beauty and goodness.

So she and the prince were married the very next morning, after which they journeyed back to the court of King Arthur, where Jack the Giant-Killer, for his many exploits, was made one of the Knights of the Round Table.

Jack the Giant-Killer

V

This, however, did not satisfy our hero, who was soon on the road again, searching for giants. He had not gone far when he came upon one, seated on a huge block of timber near the entrance to a dark cave. He was a most terrific giant. His eyes were like coals of fire, his countenance was grim and gruesome; his cheeks, like huge slabs of bacon, were covered with a stubbly beard, the bristles of which resembled rods of iron wire, while the locks of hair that fell on his brawny shoulders looked like curled snakes or hissing adders. He held a knotted iron club and breathed so heavily you could hear him a mile away.

Undaunted by this fearsome sight, Jack alighted from his horse and, putting on his coat of darkness, went close up to the giant and said softly, "Hullo! Is that you? It will not be long before I have you fast by your beard."

So saying, he made a cut at the giant's head, with the sword of strength but, somehow missing his aim, cut off the nose instead, clean as a whistle! My goodness, how the giant roared! It was like claps of thunder, and he began to slash about with the knotted iron club, like one possessed. But Jack, in his coat of darkness, easily dodged the blows, and running in behind, drove the sword up to the hilt into the giant's back, so that he fell stone dead.

Jack then cut off the head and sent it to King Arthur by a wagon driver whom he hired for the purpose. After that he began to search the giant's cave for treasure. He passed through many windings and turnings until he came to a

64

huge hall paved and roofed with limestone. At the upper
end of this was an immense fireplace where an iron cauldron
hung, bigger than any Jack had ever seen. It was boiling and
gave out a pleasing steam; beside it stood a massive table set
with huge platters and mugs. Here it was that the giants
used to dine. Going a little further he came upon a sort of
window with iron bars, and looking within he saw a vast
number of miserable captives.

"Alas! Alack!" they cried on seeing him. "Have you come,
young man, to join us in this dreadful prison?"

"That depends," said Jack. "But first tell me why you are
imprisoned?"

"Through no fault," they cried at once. "We are captives of the cruel giants and are kept here and well nourished until such time as the monsters desire a feast. Then they choose the fattest and dine on them."

On hearing this, Jack straightway unlocked the door of the prison and set the poor fellows free. Then, searching the giants' coffers, he divided the gold and silver equally among the captives as compensation for their sufferings, and taking them to a neighboring castle gave them a good feast.

VI

As they were all making merry over their deliverance and praising Jack's prowess, a messenger arrived to say that one Thunderdell, a huge giant with two heads, having heard of the death of his kinsman, was on his way from the north to seek revenge, and was already within a mile or two of the castle, the country folk with their flocks and herds flying before him like chaff before the wind.

The castle with its gardens stood on a small island that was surrounded by a moat twenty feet wide and thirty feet deep, having very steep sides. And this moat was spanned by a drawbridge. Without a moment's delay, Jack ordered the drawbridge sawn on both sides at the middle, so as to only leave one plank uncut over which he in his invisible coat of darkness passed swiftly to meet his enemy, bearing in his hand the wonderful sword of strength.

Though the giant could not see Jack, he could smell him,

for giants have keen noses. Therefore Thunderdell cried out in a voice like his name:

> "Fee, fi, fo, fum!
>   I smell the blood of an Englishman.
>   Be he alive, or be he dead,
>   I'll grind his bones to make my bread!"

"Is that so?" said Jack, cheerful as ever. "Then you are a monstrous miller for sure!"

The giant, peering round everywhere for a glimpse of his foe, shouted out, "Are you, indeed, the villain who has killed so many of my kinsmen? Then, indeed, will I tear you to pieces with my teeth, suck your blood, and grind your bones to powder."

"You will have to catch me first," said Jack, laughing. And throwing off his coat of darkness and putting on his slippers of swiftness, he began nimbly to lead the giant a pretty dance, leaping light as a feather, the monster following heavily like a walking tower, so that the very earth shook at every step. At this game the onlookers nearly split their sides with laughter, until Jack, judging there had been enough of it, made for the drawbridge, ran neatly over the single plank, and reaching the other side waited in teasing fashion for his adversary.

On came the giant at full speed, foaming at the mouth with rage, and flourishing his club. But when he came to the middle of the bridge his great weight broke the plank, and he fell headlong into the moat, rolling and wallowing like a whale, plunging from place to place, yet unable to get out and be revenged.

The spectators greeted his efforts with roars of laughter, and Jack himself was at first overcome with merriment. At last, however, he went for a rope, cast it over the giant's two heads, and with the help of a team of horses, drew them shorewards, where two blows from the sword of strength settled the matter.

VII

After a while, Jack began once more to grow restless, and taking leave of his companions, set out for fresh adventures.

He traveled far and fast, through woods, and valley, and hills, till at last he came, late at night, to a lonesome house set at the foot of a high mountain.

When he knocked at the door, it was opened by an old man whose head was white as snow.

"Sir," said Jack, courteously, "can you lodge a tired traveler?"

"Ay, that I will, and welcome to my poor cottage," replied the old man.

Whereupon Jack came in, and after supper they sat together chatting in a friendly fashion. Then the old man, seeing by Jack's belt that he was the famous giant-killer, said, "My son! You are the great conqueror of evil monsters. Now, close by there lives one well worthy of your strength.

Jack the Giant-Killer

On top of yonder high hill is an enchanted castle kept by a giant named Galligantua, who, with the help of a wicked old magician, tricks many beautiful ladies and valiant knights into the castle, where they are transformed into all sorts of birds and beasts, even into fishes and insects. There they live, confined without hope. Most of all do I grieve for a duke's daughter whom they kidnapped in her father's garden, bringing her here in a burning chariot drawn by fiery dragons. Her form is that of a white deer. Though many valiant knights have tried their best to break the spell and free her, none have succeeded; for at the entrance to the castle are two dreadful creatures who destroy everyone who attempts to pass them by."

Jack thought of the coat of darkness which had served him so well before, and he put on the cap of knowledge, and in an instant he knew what had to be done. The very next morning at dawn, Jack arose and put on his invisible coat and his slippers of swiftness. In the twinkling of an eye there he was on the top of the mountain! And there guarding the castle gates were the two horrible creatures with the bodies and hind legs of lions and the heads of eagles, with forked tails and tongues. But they could not see him because of the coat of darkness, so he passed by them unharmed.

Hung on the doors of the gateway he found a golden trumpet on a silver chain, and beneath it was engraved in red lettering:

> Whoever shall this trumpet blow
> Will cause the giant's overthrow.

Jack the Giant-Killer

The black enchantment he will break,
And gladness out of sadness make.

No sooner had Jack read these words than he put the horn to his lips and blew a loud, "Tantivy! Tantivy! Tantivy!"

At the very first note the castle trembled to its vast foundations, and before he had finished, both the giant and the magician were biting their thumbs and tearing their hair, knowing that their wickedness must now come to an end. But the giant showed fight and took up his club to defend himself, whereupon Jack, with one clean cut of the sword of strength, severed his head from his body; he would doubtless have done the same to the magician, but the latter was a coward, and, calling up a whirlwind, was swept away by it into the air, and hasn't been seen or heard of since.

The enchantments being thus broken, all the valiant knights and beautiful ladies, who had been transformed into birds and beasts and fishes and reptiles and insects, returned to their proper shapes, including the duke's daughter. From being a white deer, she now became the most beautiful maiden upon whom the sun ever shone. No sooner had this occurred than the whole castle vanished in a cloud of smoke, and from that moment giants vanished also from the land.

So Jack, when he had presented the head of Galligantua to King Arthur, together with all the lords and ladies he had delivered from enchantment, found he had nothing more to do. As a reward for past services, however, King Arthur bestowed the hand of the duke's daughter upon honest Jack the

Jack the Giant-Killer

Giant-Killer. So they were married, and the whole kingdom was filled with joy at their wedding. Furthermore, the King bestowed on Jack a noble castle with a magnificent estate, where he, his lady, and their children lived in great joy and contentment for the rest of their days.

THE THREE SILLIES

ONCE upon a time, when folk were not so wise as they are nowadays, there lived a farmer and his wife who had one daughter. And she, being a pretty lass, was courted by the young squire when he came home from his travels.

Every evening he would stroll over from the Hall to see her and stop to supper in the farmhouse, and every evening the daughter would go down into the cellar to draw the cider for supper.

One evening when she had gone down to draw the cider and had turned the tap as usual, she happened to look up at the ceiling, and there she saw a big wooden mallet stuck in one of the beams.

It must have been there for ages and ages, for it was all covered with cobwebs, but somehow or another she had never noticed it before, and she began thinking how dangerous it was to have the mallet just hanging there.

She thought to herself, "Supposing him and me was married, and supposing we was to have a son, and supposing he was to grow up to be a man, and supposing he was to come down to draw cider like I am doing, and supposing the mallet were to fall on his head and kill him, how dreadful it would be!"

With that she put down the candle she was carrying and, seating herself on a cask, began to cry. And she cried and cried and cried.

Upstairs they began to wonder why she was so long drawing the cider. After a time, her mother went down to the cellar to see what had become of her, and found her, seated on the cask, crying ever so hard, and the cider running all over the floor.

"Lawks a mercy me!" cried her mother. "Whatever is the matter?"

"O mother!" said she between her sobs, "it's that horrid mallet. Supposing him and me was married, and supposing we was to have a son, and supposing he was to grow up to be a man, and supposing he was to come down to draw cider like I am doing, and supposing the mallet were to fall on his head and kill him, how dreadful it would be!"

"Dear heart!" said the mother, seating herself beside her daughter and beginning to cry. "How dreadful it would be!"

So they both sat crying. And after a time, when they did not come back, the farmer began to wonder what had happened, and going down to the cellar found them seated side by side on the cask, crying hard, and the cider running all over the floor.

"Zounds!" said he, "Whatever is the matter?"

"Just look at that horrid mallet up there, father," moaned the mother. "Supposing our daughter was to marry her sweetheart, and supposing they was to have a son, and supposing he was to grow up to be a man, and supposing he was to come down to draw cider like we are doing, and supposing that there mallet was to fall on his head and kill him, how dreadful it would be!"

"Dreadful indeed!" said the father and, seating himself beside his wife and daughter, started crying, too.

Now upstairs the young squire wanted his supper. At last he lost patience and went down into the cellar to see for himself what they were doing. And there he found them seated side by side on the cask crying, with their feet awash in cider, for the floor was flooded. So the first thing he did was to run and turn off the tap. Then he said, "What are you three doing, sitting there crying like babies, and letting good cider run over the floor?"

Then they all three began to talk at once, "Look at that horrid mallet! Supposing you and $\frac{me}{she}$ was married, and supposing $\frac{we}{you}$ had a son, and supposing he was to grow up to be a man, and supposing he was to come down here to draw cider like we are, and supposing that there mallet was to fall down on his head and kill him, how dreadful it would be!"

Then the young squire burst out laughing and laughed till he was tired. But at last he reached up to the old mallet and pulled it out, and put it safely on the floor. And he shook his head and said, "I've traveled far and I've traveled fast, but never have I met with three such sillies as you three. I can't marry one of the three biggest sillies in the world. So I shall start again on my travels, and if I can find three bigger sillies than you three, then I'll come back and be married—not otherwise."

So he wished them good-bye and started again on his travels, leaving them all crying; this time because the marriage was off!

The young man traveled far and he traveled fast, but never did he find a bigger silly, until one day he came upon an old woman's cottage that had some grass growing on the thatched roof.

The old woman was trying her best to coax her cow into going up a ladder to eat the grass. But the poor thing was afraid and wouldn't go. Then the old woman tried poking it with a stick, but it wouldn't go. You never saw such a sight! The cow was getting more and more flustered and obstinate, and the old woman was getting hotter and hotter.

At last the young squire said, "It would be easier if *you* went up the ladder, cut the grass, and threw it down for the cow to eat."

"A likely story," said the old woman. "A cow can cut grass for herself. And the foolish thing will be quite safe up there, for I'll tie a rope round her neck, pass the rope down the chimney, and fasten the other end to my wrist, so when I'm doing my bit of washing, she can't fall off the roof without my knowing it. So mind your own business, young sir."

After a while the old woman coaxed and codgered and bullied and badgered the cow up the ladder, and when she got it onto the roof she tied a rope round its neck, passed the rope down the chimney, and fastened the other end to her wrist.

Then she went about her bit of washing, and the young squire went on his way.

He hadn't gone but a bit when he heard the awfullest hullabaloo. He galloped back, and found that the cow had fallen off the roof and got strangled by the rope round its neck, while the weight of the cow had pulled the old woman by her wrist up the chimney, where she had got stuck halfway and been smothered by the soot!

"That is one bigger silly," said the young squire as he journeyed on. "So now to find two more!"

He did not find any, however, till late one night he arrived at a little inn. And the inn was so full that he had to share a room with another traveler. His roommate proved to be a pleasant fellow, and each slept well in his bed.

But next morning, when they were dressing, what did the stranger do but carefully hang his trousers on the knobs of the tall chest of drawers!

"What are you doing?" asked the young squire.

"I'm putting on my trousers," said the stranger; and he went to the other end of the room, took a little run, and tried to jump into the trousers.

But he didn't succeed, so he took another run and another try, and another and another and another, until he got quite hot and flustered, as the old woman had got over her cow that wouldn't go up the ladder. And all the time the young squire was laughing fit to split, for never in his life did he see anything so comical.

Then the stranger stopped and mopped his face with his handkerchief, for he was all in a sweat. "It's very well for you to laugh," said he, "but trousers are the most awkward things to get into that ever were. It takes me the best part of an hour every morning before I get them on. How do you manage yours?"

Then the young squire showed him, as well as he could for he was still laughing, how to put on his trousers, and the stranger was very grateful and said he never should have thought of it that way.

"So that," said the young squire to himself, "is a second bigger silly." But he traveled far and he traveled fast without finding the third, until one bright night when the moon was shining overhead he came upon a village. And outside the village was a pond, and round about the pond was a great crowd of villagers. And some had rakes, and some had pitchforks, and some had brooms. And they were as busy as busy could be, shouting out, and raking, and forking, and sweeping away at the pond.

"What is the matter?" cried the young squire, jumping off his horse to help. "Has someone fallen in?"

"Aye!" said they. "Can't you see the moon's fallen into the pond, and we can't get her out nohow."

And with that they set again to raking, and forking, and sweeping away. Then the young squire burst out laughing, told them they were fools for their pains, and told them to look up over their heads where the moon was riding broad and full. But they wouldn't, and they wouldn't believe that what they saw in the water was only a reflection. When he insisted they threatened to duck him in the pond. So he got on his horse again as quickly as he could, leaving them raking, and forking, and sweeping away; and for all we know they may be at it yet!

But the young squire said to himself, "There are many more sillies in this world than I thought, so I'll just go back and marry the farmer's daughter. She is no sillier than the rest."

So they were married, and if they didn't live happily ever after, that has nothing to do with the story of the three sillies.

"O Tree of mine! Have you seen my naughty little maid?"
Page 87

He climbed, and he climbed, and he climbed
Page 93

THE TWO SISTERS

ONCE upon a time there were two sisters who were as much like each other as two peas in a pod; but one was nice, and the other was bad-tempered. Times were hard and their father had no work, so the girls began to think of hiring out as servants.

"I will go first and see what I can do," said the younger sister, cheerfully. "Then you, sis, can follow if I have good luck."

So she packed up a bundle, said good-bye, and started out to find a job. But no one in the town wanted a housekeeper, and she went farther afield into the country. And as she journeyed she came upon an oven in which a lot of loaves were baking. As she passed, the loaves cried out with one voice, "Little girl! Little girl! Take us out! Please take us out! We have been baking for seven years, and no one has come to take us out. Do take us out or we shall soon be burnt!"

Being a kind, obliging girl, she stopped, put down her bundle, took out the bread, and went on her way saying, "You will be more comfortable now."

After a time she came to a cow mooing beside an empty pail, and the cow said to her, "Little girl! Little girl! Milk me! Please milk me! Seven years have I been waiting, but no one has come to milk me!"

The Two Sisters

The kind girl stopped, put down her bundle, milked the cow into the pail, and went on her way saying, "Now you will be more comfortable."

By and by she came to an apple tree so heavy with fruit that its branches were almost breaking, and the apple tree called to her, "Little girl! Little girl! Please shake my branches. The fruit weighs me down so I can't stand straight!"

Then the kind girl stopped, put down her bundle, and shook the branches so that the apples fell off, and the tree could stand straight. Then she went on her way saying, "You will be more comfortable now."

And she journeyed on till she came to a house where an old witch lived. Now this witch wanted a maid servant and promised good wages. Therefore, the girl agreed to stop with her and see how she liked keeping house for the witch. She had to sweep the floor, keep the house clean and tidy, the fire bright and cheery. But there was one thing the witch said she must never do, and that was look up the chimney!

"If you do," said the witch, "something will fall down on you, and you will come to a bad end."

Well, the girl swept and dusted and made the fire; but was never paid a penny of wages. Now the girl wanted to go home as she did not like keeping house for the witch because this was a nasty witch who frightened all the children who came near and stole their pennies and treats. But the girl did not like to go home penniless, so she stayed on, sweeping and dusting and doing her work, just as if she was pleased. Then one day as she was sweeping up the hearth, down tumbled some soot and, without remembering she was forbidden to look up the chimney, she looked up to see where the soot came from. And, lo and behold! A big bag of gold fell right into her lap.

Now the witch happened to be out on one of her errands, so the girl thought it was a fine opportunity to be off home.

So she grabbed up her few things and started to run home; but she had only gone a little way when she heard the witch coming after her on her broomstick. Now the apple tree she had helped to stand straight happened to be quite close; so she ran to it and cried:

> "Apple tree! Apple tree, hide me
> So the old witch can't find me,
> For if she does she'll curse and beat me,
> And prison me in her cold, dark pantry."

Then the apple tree said, "Of course I will. You helped me to stand straight, and one good turn deserves another."

So the apple tree hid her nicely in its green branches. When the witch flew past asking:

> "Tree of mine! O Tree of mine!
> Have you seen my naughty little maid
> With a willy willy wag and a great big bag,
> She's stolen my money—all I had?"

the apple tree answered:

> "No, mother dear,
> Not for seven year!"

The Two Sisters

So the witch flew on the wrong way, and the girl got down, thanked the tree politely, and started home again. But just as she got to where the cow was standing beside the pail, she heard the witch coming again, so she ran to the cow and cried:

> "Cow! Cow, please hide me
> So the witch can't find me;
> If she does she'll curse and beat me,
> And prison me in her cold, dark pantry."

"Certainly I will," answered the cow. "Didn't you milk me and make me comfortable? Hide yourself behind me and you'll be quite safe."

And when the witch flew by and called to the cow:

> "O Cow of mine! Cow of mine!
> Have you seen my naughty little maid
> With a willy willy wag and a great big bag,
> Who stole my money—all that I had?"

she just said politely:

> "No, mother dear,
> Not for seven year!"

Then the old witch went on in the wrong direction and the girl started again on her way home, but just as she got to where the oven stood, she heard the awful old witch coming behind her again, so she ran as fast as she could to the oven and cried:

The Two Sisters

"O Oven! Oven! Hide me
So the witch can't find me,
For if she does she'll curse and beat me,
And prison me in her cold, dark pantry."

Then the oven said, "I am afraid there is no room for you, since another batch of bread is baking, but there is the baker—ask him."

So she asked the baker, and he said, "Of course I will. You saved my last batch from being burnt, so run into the bakery. You will be quite safe there and I will settle the witch for you."

So she hid in the bakery, only just in time, for there was the old witch calling angrily:

"O Man of mine! Man of mine!
Have you seen my naughty little maid
With a willy willy wag and a great big bag,
Who's stole my money—all I had?"

Then the baker replied, "Look in the oven. She may be there."

And the witch climbed down from her broomstick and peered into the oven, but she could see no one.

"Creep in and look in the farthest corner," said the baker slyly, and the witch crept in, when—Bang!—he shut the door in her face, and there she was baking. And when she came out with the bread she was all crisp and brown, and had to go home as best she could and put cold cream all over her!

But the kind, obliging girl got home safely with her bag of money.

Now the ill-tempered elder sister was very jealous of this good luck, and determined to get a bag of gold for herself. So she in her turn packed up a bundle and started to seek her fortune by the same road. But when she came to the oven, and the loaves begged her to take them out because they had been baking seven years and were almost burning, she tossed her head and said, "A likely story indeed, that I should burn my fingers to save your crusts. No, thank you!"

And with that she went on till she came across the cow standing waiting to be milked beside the pail. But when the cow said, "Little girl! Little girl! Milk me! Please milk me, I've waited seven years to be milked—"

She only laughed and replied, "You may wait another seven years for all I care. I'm not your dairymaid!"

And with that she went on till she came to the apple tree, which was weighed down by its fruit. But when it begged her to shake its branches, she only giggled, and plucking one ripe apple, said, "One is enough for me. You can keep the rest yourself."

And with that she went on munching the apple, till she came to the witch's house.

Now the witch, though she had gotten over being baked in the oven, was dreadfully angry with all little girls, and she made up her mind that this one should not trick her. So for a long time she never went out of the house and the bad-tempered sister never had a chance to look up the chimney, as she had meant to do at once. She had to dust and clean and brush and sweep ever so hard until she was quite tired out.

But one day when the witch went into the garden, the girl seized the moment, looked up the chimney and, sure enough, a bag of gold fell right into her lap!

Well, she was off with it in a moment, and ran and ran till she came to the apple tree, when she heard the witch behind her. So she cried as her sister had done:

> "Apple tree! Apple tree, hide me
> So the old witch can't find me,
> For if she does she'll curse and beat me,
> And prison me in her cold, dark pantry."

But the apple tree said, "No room here! I've too many apples."

So she had to run on, and when the witch on her broomstick came flying by and called:

> "O Tree of mine! Tree of mine!
> Have you seen a naughty little maid
> With a willy willy wag and a great big bag,
> Who's stolen my money—all I had?"

the apple tree replied:

> "Yes, mother dear,
> She's gone down there."

Then the witch went after her, caught her, took the bag of money away from her, and sent her home without a penny payment for all her dusting and sweeping and brushing and cleaning.

JACK AND THE BEANSTALK

A LONG long time ago, when most of the world was young, there lived a boy called Jack.

His father was bedridden, and his mother, a good soul, was busy from early morning till late evening planning how to support her sick husband and her young son by selling the milk and butter which Milky White, the beautiful cow, generously gave them. When winter came on, the plants of the fields took refuge from the frosts in the warm earth, and though his mother sent Jack to gather what he could, he came back as often as not with a very empty sack, for Jack's eyes were so often full of wonder at all the things he saw that sometimes he forgot to work!

It came to pass that one morning Milky White gave no milk at all—not one drop! Then the good hard-working mother threw her apron over her head and sobbed, "What shall we do? What shall we do?"

Now Jack loved his mother; besides, he felt just a bit guilty at being such a big boy and doing so little to help, so he said, "Cheer up! Cheer up! I'll go and get work somewhere." And he felt as if he would work his fingers to the bone; but the good woman shook her head mournfully.

"You've tried that before, Jack," she said, "and nobody hired you. You are a good lad but your wits go woolgathering.

No, we must sell Milky White and live on the money. It is no use crying over milk that is not here to spill!"

You see, she was a wise as well as a hard-working woman, and Jack's spirits rose.

"You're right," he cried. "We will sell Milky White and be richer than ever. It's an ill wind that blows no one good. So, as it is market day, I'll take her there and we shall see what we shall see."

"But——" began his mother.

"But doesn't butter parsnips," laughed Jack. "Trust me to make a good bargain."

So, as it was washing day, and her sick husband was more ailing than usual, his mother let Jack set off to sell the cow.

"Not less than ten pounds," she called after him as he turned the corner.

Ten pounds, indeed! Jack had made up his mind to sell the cow for twenty! Twenty solid golden sovereigns!

As he was going along he saw a little old man on the road who called out, "Good morning, Jack!"

"Good morning," replied Jack, with a polite bow, wondering how the little old man happened to know his name; though, to be sure, boys named Jack were as plentiful as blackberries.

"And where may you be going?" asked the little old man. Jack wondered again why the little old man wanted to know, but, being always polite, he replied, "I am going to market to sell Milky White—and I mean to make a good bargain."

"So you will! So you will!" chuckled the little old man.

"You look a bright sort of chap. I bet you know how many beans make five?"

"Two in each hand and one in my mouth," answered Jack readily. He really was sharp as a needle.

"That's right!" chuckled the little old man; and as he spoke he drew out of his pocket five beans. "Well, here they are, so give us Milky White."

Jack was so flabbergasted that he stood with his mouth open as if he expected the fifth bean to fly into it.

"What!" he said at last. "My Milky White for five common beans! Certainly not!"

"But they aren't common beans," said the little old man, and there was an odd little smile on his odd little face. "If you plant these beans at night, by morning they will have grown up right into the very sky."

Jack was too flabbergasted this time even to open his mouth, but his eyes opened wide. "Did you say right into the very sky?" he asked at last.

"RIGHT UP INTO THE VERY SKY," repeated the little old man, with a nod between each word. "It's a good bargain, Jack; and if they don't grow so high—why, meet me here tomorrow morning and you shall have Milky White back again. Will that please you?"

"Right as rain," cried Jack, without stopping to think, and the next moment he found himself standing on an empty road.

"Two in each hand and one in my mouth," repeated Jack. "That is what I said, and what I'll do. And if what the little old man said isn't true, I shall get Milky White back tomorrow morning."

So whistling and munching the bean in his mouth he trudged home cheerfully, wondering what the sky would be like if he ever got there.

"What a long time you've been!" exclaimed his mother, who was anxiously watching for him at the gate. "It is past sunset, but I see you have sold Milky White. Tell me quick how much you got for her."

"You'll never guess," began Jack.

"Laws-a-mercy! You don't say so," interrupted the good woman. "And I worrying all day lest they should trick you. What was it? Ten pounds—fifteen—sure it *can't* be twenty!"

Jack held out the beans triumphantly.

Jack and the Beanstalk

"There," he said. "That's what I got for her, and a jolly good bargain too!"

It was his mother's turn to be flabbergasted, but all she said was, "What! Beans?"

"Yes," replied Jack, beginning to doubt his own wisdom; "but they're *magic* beans. If you plant them at night, by morning they—grow—right up—into—the—sky—Oh! Please don't hit so hard!"

For Jack's mother for once had lost her temper, and was swatting the boy for all she was worth with her broom. And when she had finished scolding, she flung the miserable beans out of window and sent him to bed without supper.

If this was the magical effect of the beans, thought Jack, he didn't want any more magic, if you please.

However, being healthy and, as a rule, happy, he soon fell asleep and slept like a top.

When he woke he thought at first it was moonlight, for everything in the room glowed greenish. Then he stared at the little window. It was covered by a curtain of leaves. He was out of bed in a trice, and the next moment, without waiting to dress, was climbing up the biggest beanstalk you ever saw. For what the strange little old man had said was true! One of the beans which his mother had chucked into the garden had found soil, taken root, and grown in the night. . . .

Where? Up to the very sky? Jack meant to see at any rate.

So he climbed and he climbed and he climbed. It was easy work, for the big beanstalk with the leaves growing out of each side was like a ladder. Even so, he soon was out of breath. Then he got his second wind, and was just beginning to wonder if he had a third when he saw in front of him a wide, shining white road stretching away and away and away.

So he took to walking, and he walked and walked and walked, till he came to a tall, shining white house with a wide white doorstep.

And on the doorstep stood a great big woman with a black kettle full of porridge in her hand. Now Jack, having had no supper, was hungry as a hunter, and when he saw the porridge-pot he said quite politely, "Good morning, ma'am. I wonder if you could give me some breakfast?"

"Breakfast!" echoed the woman, who was really an ogre's wife. "If it is breakfast you're wanting, it's breakfast you'll likely be, for I expect my man home any minute, and there is nothing he likes better for breakfast than a fat little boy."

Now Jack was not a bit of a coward, and when he wanted a thing he generally got it, so he said cheerfully, "I'd be fatter if I'd had my breakfast!" The ogre's wife laughed and told Jack to come in, for she was not really half as bad as she looked. But he had hardly finished the great bowl of porridge and milk she gave him when the whole house began to tremble and quake. It was the ogre coming home!

Thump! THUMP!! THUMP!!!

"Into the oven with you, quick!" cried the ogre's wife; and the oven door was just closed when the ogre strode in. Jack could see him through the little peephole slide at the top of the oven where the steam came out.

He was a big one for sure. He had three sheep strung to his

belt, and he threw them down on the table. "Here, wife," he cried. "Roast me these snippets for breakfast. They are all I've been able to get this morning, worse luck! I hope the oven's hot!" And he went to touch the handle, while Jack burst out in a sweat, wondering what would happen next.

"Roast!" echoed the ogre's wife. "Pooh! Better to boil them."

So she set to work to cook them, but the ogre began sniffing about the room. Then he frowned horribly and began the real ogre's rhyme:

"Fee-fi-fo-fum,
I smell the blood of an Englishman.
Be he alive, or be he dead,
I'll grind his bones to make my bread."

"Don't be silly!" said his wife. "There's no one here. Come, eat your breakfast, there's a good ogre!"

So the ogre ate his three sheep, and when he had finished he went to a big oak chest and took out three big bags of golden coins. He put the bags on the table, and began to count the coins while his wife cleared away the breakfast things. And by and by his head began to nod, and at last he began to snore, and snored so loud that the whole house shook.

Then Jack nipped out of the oven and, seizing one of the bags of gold, crept away, and ran along the straight, wide, shining white road as fast as his legs would carry him till he came to the beanstalk. He couldn't climb down it with the heavy bag of gold, so he just flung his burden down first and climbed, helter-skelter, after it.

When he came to the bottom, there was his mother picking up gold pieces out of the garden as fast as she could, for, of course, the bag had burst.

"Laws-a-mercy me!" she said. "Wherever have you been? See! It's been raining gold!"

"No, it hasn't," began Jack. "I climbed up—" Then he turned to look for the beanstalk; but, lo and behold! It wasn't there at all! So he knew, then, it was all real magic.

After that they lived happily on the gold pieces for a long time, and the bedridden father got all sorts of nice things to eat. But, at last, a day came when Jack's mother showed a sad face as she put a big gold sovereign into Jack's hand and told him to be careful marketing, because it was the last one. After that they must starve.

That night Jack chose to go to bed without any supper. If he couldn't make money, he thought, at any rate he could eat less. It was a shame for a big boy to stuff himself and bring no food to the house.

He slept like a top, as boys do when they don't overeat, and when he woke . . . presto! The whole room glowed greenish, and there was a curtain of leaves over the window! Another bean had grown in the night, and Jack climbed up it quick as he could go.

This time he didn't take nearly so long climbing until he reached the straight, wide, white road, and in a trice he found himself before the tall white house, where on the wide white steps the ogre's wife was standing with the black porridge pot in her hand.

This time Jack was as bold as brass. "Good morning, ma'am," he said. "I've come to ask you for breakfast, for I had no supper, and I'm as hungry as a hunter."

"Go away, bad boy!" replied the ogre's wife. "Last time I gave a boy breakfast my man missed a whole bag of gold. I believe you are the same boy."

"Maybe I am, maybe I'm not," said Jack, with a laugh. "I'll tell you true when I've had my breakfast, but not till then."

So the ogre's wife, who was dreadfully curious, gave him a big bowl full of porridge; but before he had half finished it he heard the ogre coming—

Thump! THUMP! THUMP!

"In with you to the oven," shrieked the ogre's wife.

This time Jack saw through the steam peephole that the ogre had three fat cows strung to his belt.

"Better luck today, wife!" he cried, and his voice shook the house. "Quick! Roast these trifles for my breakfast! I hope the oven's hot!"

And he went to feel the handle of the door, but his wife cried out sharply, "Roast! Why, you'd have to wait hours before they were done! I'll broil them—see how bright the fire is!"

"Umph!" growled the ogre. And then he began sniffing and calling out:

Jack and the Beanstalk

"Fee-fi-fo-fum,
I smell the blood of an Englishman.
Be he alive, or be he dead,
I'll grind his bones to make my bread."

"Twaddle!" said the ogre's wife. "It's only the leftovers from last night's dinner."

"Umph!" said the ogre harshly; but he ate the broiled meat, and then he said to his wife, "Bring me my hen that lays the magic eggs. I want to see gold."

So the ogre's wife brought him a great big black hen with a shiny red comb. She plumped it down on the table and took away the breakfast things.

Then the ogre said to the hen, "Lay!" and it promptly laid —what do you think?—a beautiful, shiny, yellow, golden egg!

"Henny-penny," laughed the ogre, "I shan't have to beg as long as I've got you." Then he said once more, "Lay!" And, lo and behold! There was another beautiful, shiny, yellow, golden egg!

Jack could hardly believe his eyes, and made up his mind that he would have that hen, come what might. When the ogre began to doze, he popped out of the oven in a flash, seized the hen, and ran for his life! But, you see, he reckoned without his prize; for hens, you know, always cackle when they leave their nests after laying an egg, and this one set up such a screeching that it woke the ogre.

"Where's my hen?" he shouted, and his wife came rushing in, and they both rushed to the door; but Jack had gotten a good start, and all they could see was a little figure running away down the wide white road, holding a big, screeching, cackling, fluttering black hen by the legs!

How Jack got down the beanstalk he never knew. It was all wings, and leaves, and feathers, and cacklings; but get down he did, and there was his mother wondering if the sky was going to fall!

But the very moment Jack touched ground he called out, "Lay!" and the black hen ceased cackling and laid a great, big, shiny, yellow, golden egg.

So everyone was satisfied; and from that moment everybody had everything that money could buy. For, whenever they wanted anything, they just said, "Lay!" and the black hen provided them with gold.

But soon Jack began to wonder if he couldn't find something else besides money in the sky. So one fine moonlight midsummer night he refused his supper, and before he went to bed stole out to the garden with a big watering can and watered the ground under his window. He thought, "There must be two more beans somewhere, and perhaps it is too dry for them to grow." Then he slept like a top.

And, lo and behold! When he awoke, there was the green light shimmering through his room, and in an instant he was on the beanstalk, climbing, climbing, climbing for all he was worth.

But this time he knew better than to ask for his breakfast, for the ogre's wife would be sure to recognize him. So he hid in some bushes beside the great white house, till he saw her in the kitchen, and then he slipped out and hid himself in the copper kettle, for he knew she would be sure to look in the oven first thing.

And by and by he heard—

Thump! THUMP! THUMP!

And peeping through a crack in the copper lid, he could see the ogre stalk in with three huge oxen strung at his belt. This time, no sooner had the ogre got into the house than he began shouting:

"Fee-fi-fo-fum,
I smell the blood of an Englishman.
Be he alive, or be he dead,
I'll grind his bones to make my bread."

For, see you, the copper lid didn't fit tight like the oven door, and ogres have noses like a dog's for scent.

"Well, I declare, so do I!" exclaimed the ogre's wife. "It must be that horrid boy who stole the bag of gold and the hen. If so, he's hiding in the oven!"

But when she opened the door, lo and behold! Jack wasn't there! Only some joints of meat were roasting and sizzling away. Then she laughed and said, "You and me are fools for sure. So eat your breakfast, there's a good ogre!"

But the ogre, though he enjoyed his meal very much, wasn't satisfied, and every now and then he would burst out with *"Fee-fi-fo-fum,"* and get up and search the cupboards, keeping Jack in a fever of fear lest he should think of looking in the copper kettle.

But he didn't. And when he had finished his breakfast he called out to his wife, "Bring me my magic harp! I want to be amused."

So she brought out a little harp and put it on the table. And the ogre leant back in his chair and said lazily, "Sing!"

And the harp began to sing. And it sang so beautifully that Jack forgot to be frightened, and the ogre forgot to think of *"Fee-fi-fo-fum,"* and fell asleep and did NOT SNORE!

Then Jack stole out of the copper kettle like a mouse and crept on his hands and knees to the table, raised himself up ever so softly and took hold of the magic harp.

No sooner had he touched it, than it cried out quite loud, "Master! Master!" The ogre awoke, saw Jack making off, and rushed after him.

My goodness, it was a race! Jack was nimble, but the ogre's stride was twice as long. Though Jack turned, and twisted, and doubled back like a rabbit, when he got to the beanstalk, the ogre was only a dozen yards behind him. Without time to think, Jack flung himself onto the stalk and began to go down as fast as he could, while the harp kept calling, "Master! Master!" at the top of its voice. He had only got down about a quarter of the way when there was the most awful lurch you can think of, and Jack nearly fell off the beanstalk. It was the ogre beginning to climb down, and his weight made the stalk sway like a tree in a storm. Jack knew it was life or death, and he climbed down faster and faster, and as he climbed he shouted, "Mother! Mother! Bring an axe! Bring an axe!"

Jack and the Beanstalk

As luck would have it, his mother was in the backyard chopping wood, and she ran out thinking that this time the sky must have fallen. Just at that moment Jack touched ground and flung down the harp—which immediately began to sing of all sorts of beautiful things. He seized the axe and gave a great chop at the beanstalk, which shook and swayed and bent like wheat before a breeze.

"Be careful!" shouted the ogre, clinging on as hard as he could. But Jack *was* careful, and he dealt that beanstalk such a blow that all of it, ogre and all, came toppling down and, of course, the ogre broke his neck and died on the spot.

After that everyone was quite happy. They had gold to spare, and if the bedridden father was weak, Jack brought out the harp and said, "Sing!" And it sang about everything under the sun.

Jack ceased wondering so much and became quite a useful person.

And the last bean hasn't grown yet. It is still in the garden.

I wonder if it will ever grow? And what little child will climb its beanstalk into the sky? And what will that child find?

Oh, goodness me!

THE BLACK BULL OF NORROWAY

LONG ago in Norroway there lived a lady who had three pretty daughters of marriageable age. One night the daughters began to talk about whom they meant to marry.

The eldest said, "I will have no one lower than an Earl."

And the second said, "I will have none lower than a Lord."

But the third, the prettiest and the merriest, tossed her head and said, with a twinkle in her eye, "Why so proud? As for me I would be content with the Black Bull of Norroway."

At that the other sisters told her to be silent and not talk lightly of such a monster. For they had all heard:

> To wilder measures now they turn,
> The black black Bull of Norroway;
> Suddenly the candles cease to burn,
> The minstrels cease to play.

And everyone thought the Black Bull of Norroway was a horrible monster.

But the youngest daughter would have her laugh, so she said three times that she would be content with the Black Bull of Norroway.

It so happened that the very next morning a coach drawn

by six horses came swinging along the road, and in it sat an Earl who had come to ask for the hand of the eldest daughter in marriage. There was great rejoicing over the wedding and the bride and bridegroom drove away in the coach-and-six.

Then the next thing that happened was that a coach drawn by four horses with a Lord in it came swinging along the road and he wanted to marry the second daughter. So they were wed, and there was great rejoicing, and the bride and bridegroom drove away in the coach-and-four.

Now, after this there was only the youngest, the prettiest and the merriest, of the sisters left, and she became the apple of her mother's eye. So you may imagine how the mother felt when one morning a terrible bellowing was heard at the door, and there was a great big Black Bull waiting for his bride.

She wept and she wailed and at first the girl ran away and hid herself in the cellar, but there the Bull stood waiting and at last the girl came up and said, "I promised I would be content with the Black Bull of Norroway and I must keep my word. Farewell, mother, you will not see me again."

Then she mounted the Black Bull's back, and it walked quietly away with her. And the Black Bull chose the smoothest paths and the easiest roads, so that at last the girl grew less afraid. But she became very hungry and was almost fainting when the Black Bull said to her, in a soft voice that wasn't a bellow at all:

"Eat out of my left ear,
Drink out of my right,

The Black Bull of Norroway

And save what you leave
To serve tomorrow night."

So she did as she was told, and, lo and behold, the left ear was full of delicious things to eat, and the right was full of the most delicious drinks, and there was plenty left over for several days.

And so they journeyed on, and journeyed on through many dreadful forests and many lonely wastes and the Black Bull never paused to eat or sleep, but the girl he carried ate out of his left ear and drank out of his right and saved what was left to eat the following evening. And she slept soft and warm on his broad back.

After days of travel they reached a magnificent castle where a large company of lords and ladies were assembled. They wondered at the sight of these strange companions, but they invited the girl to supper, and they turned the Black Bull into the field, leaving him to spend the night with his own kind.

When the next morning came, the Black Bull was ready for his burden again, and although the girl did not want to leave her pleasant companions, she remembered her promise and mounted on his back. They journeyed on, and journeyed on, and journeyed on, through many tangled woods and over many high mountains. And the Black Bull always chose the smoothest paths and pushed aside the briars and brambles, and she ate out of his left ear and drank out of his right.

At last they came to a magnificent mansion where dukes and duchesses and earls and countesses were enjoying themselves. The company was greatly surprised at the strange companions but they asked the girl in to supper and they would have turned the Black Bull into the park for the night, but the girl, remembering how well he had cared for her, asked them to put him into the stable and give him a good feed.

So this was done, and the next morning he was waiting before the hall door for his burden; and although she regretted leaving the fine company, she mounted him cheerfully enough, and they rode away, and they rode away, and they rode away, through thick briars and up fearsome cliffs. And always the Black Bull trod the brambles underfoot and chose the easiest paths, while she ate out of his left ear and drank out of his right, and wanted for nothing, though he neither ate nor drank. It came to pass that he grew tired and was limping with one foot when, just as the sun was setting, they came to a beautiful palace where princes and princesses were playing games on the green grass. And though they wondered a good deal at the strange companions, they asked the girl to join them, and ordered the grooms to take the Black Bull to a field.

But she, remembering all he had done for her, said, "No!" He will stay with me!" Then seeing a large thorn in the foot on which he had been limping, she stooped down and pulled it out.

And lo and behold, in an instant, to everyone's surprise, there appeared not a frightful monstrous bull, but one of the most beautiful princes anyone had ever seen. He fell at his deliverer's feet, thanking her for having broken his cruel enchantment.

A wicked witch who wanted to marry him had, he said, cast a spell on him until a beautiful maiden of her own free will should do him a favor.

The Black Bull of Norroway

"But," he said, "the danger is not all over. You have broken the enchantment by night; that by day has yet to be overcome."

So the next morning the prince had to resume the form of a bull, and they set out together; and they rode, and they rode, and they rode, till they came to a dark forbidding glen. And here he asked her to dismount and sit on a great rock.

"Here you must stay," he said, "while I go and fight the Old One. But be careful! Move neither hand nor foot while I am away, or else I shall never find you again. If everything around you turns blue, I shall have beaten the Old One, but if everything turns red, he will have defeated me."

And with that, and a tremendous roaring bellow, he set off to find his foe.

Well, she sat as still as a mouse, moving neither hand nor foot, not even her eyes, and waited and waited and waited. Then at last everything turned blue. But she was so overcome with joy to think that her lover was victorious that she forgot to keep still, and lifting one of her feet, crossed it over the other.

So she waited and waited and waited. She sat for a long time and she grew weary. And all the time he was looking for her, but he never found her.

Finally she decided to leave that place and search for her lover through the whole wide world. She journeyed on and she journeyed on and she journeyed on, until one day in the dark woods she came to a little hut where an old, old woman gave her food and shelter and bid her godspeed on her errand, giving her three nuts: a walnut, a filbert, and a hazelnut, with these words:

"When your heart is like to break,
And once again is like to break,
Crack a nut and in its shell
That will be that suits you well."

After this she felt heartened and she wandered on till the road was blocked by a great hill of glass; and as hard as she tried to climb it, she could not. She slipped back and slipped back and slipped back, for it was like ice.

So she looked for another way. Round and round the foot of the hill she went, sobbing and wailing, but she could find no way. At last she came to a blacksmith's shop, and the smith promised if she would serve him faithfully for seven years and seven days, he would make her iron shoes with which to climb the hill of glass. So for seven long years and seven short days she toiled and swept and washed in the smith's house. And for wages he gave her a pair of iron shoes and with them she climbed the glassy hill and went on her way.

She had not gone far before a company of lords and ladies rode past her, talking of the goings on at the young Duke of Norroway's wedding. Then she passed a number of people carrying all sorts of good things which they told her were for the Duke's wedding. And at last she came to a castle where the courtyards were full of cooks and bakers, some running this way, some running that, and all so busy that they did not know what to do first.

The Black Bull of Norroway

Then she heard the horns of hunters and cries of "Make way! Make way for the Duke of Norroway and his bride!"

And who should ride past but the beautiful prince who had been her Black Bull and by his side was the witch who was determined to marry him that very day.

At the sight she felt that her heart would break. The time had come for her to crack one of the nuts. She broke the walnut, since it was the biggest and out of it came a wonderful small woman cleaning wool as fast as she could.

Now when the witch saw this wonderful thing, she offered the girl her choice of anything in the castle for it.

"If you will put off your wedding with the Duke for a day, and let me watch in his room tonight," said the girl, "you shall have it."

Now, like all witches, the bride wanted everything her own way and she was so sure she had her groom safe that she consented. But before the Duke went to bed she gave him a drink made with her own hands that would put to sleep anyone who drank it till morning.

So, although the girl was allowed alone in the Duke's chamber and even though she spent the night sighing and singing:

"Far have I searched for you,
  Long have I worked for you,
  Near am I brought to you,
  Dear Duke of Norroway;
  Will you say nothing to me?"

111

the Duke never awakened, but slept on. So when day came the girl had to leave him without his ever knowing she had been there.

Then once again her heart was breaking over and over again so she cracked the filbert nut, because it was the next biggest. And out of it came a wonderful tiny woman spinning away as fast as she could spin. Now when the witch saw this wonderful thing she once again put off her wedding so that she might possess it. And once again the girl spent the night in the Duke's chamber sighing and singing:

> "Far have I searched for you,
>   Long have I worked for you,
>   Near am I brought to you,
>   Dear Duke of Norroway;
>   Will you say nothing to me?"

But the Duke, who had drunk the sleeping potion from the hands of his bride, never stirred, and when dawn came the girl had to leave without his knowing she had been there.

Then, again, the girl's heart was breaking over and over and over again, so she cracked the last nut—the hazelnut—and out of it came the tiniest tiniest woman weaving away at yarn as fast as she could weave.

And this marvel so delighted the witch that once again she consented to put off her wedding for a day, and allow the girl to watch in the Duke's chamber the night through.

Now it so happened that when the Duke was dressing that morning he heard his pages talking among themselves about

She went along and went along and went along
Page 116

Mr. and Mrs. Vinegar at home
Page 127

the strange sighing and singing they had heard in the night and he said to his faithful old valet, "What do the pages mean?"

And the old valet, who hated the witch, said, "If the master takes no drink tonight, he may also hear what for two nights has kept me awake."

The Duke was greatly interested in this and when his bride-to-be brought him his evening drink, he said it was not sweet enough, and while she went away to get honey to sweeten it, he poured away the drink and made believe he had swallowed it.

So that night when darkness came, and the girl stole into his chamber with a heavy heart thinking it would be the very last time she would ever see him, the Duke was really wide awake. And when she sat down by his bedside and began to sing:

"Far have I searched for thee,"

he knew her voice at once, and clasped her in his arms.

Then he told her how he had been in the power of the witch and had forgotten everything, but that now he remembered all and that the spell was broken forever.

So the wedding feast was for their marriage, since the witch, seeing her power was gone, quickly fled the country and was never heard of again.

CATSKIN

ONCE upon a time there lived a gentleman who owned fine lands and houses, and he very much wanted to have a son to be heir to them. So when his wife brought him a daughter, though she was as pretty as could be, he cared nothing for her, and said, "Let me never see her face."

She grew up to be a beautiful maiden, although her father never set eyes on her till she was eighteen years old and was ready to be married.

Then her father said roughly, "She shall marry the first man that comes for her." When this news became known, who should come along and be first but a nasty, horrid old man! The maiden didn't know what to do, and went for advice to the hen-wife, who cared for the fowls. She said, "Say you will not take him unless he gives you a coat of silver cloth." He gave her a coat of silver cloth, but she still wouldn't take him, but went again to the hen-wife, who said, "Say you will not take him unless he gives you a coat of beaten gold." Well, he gave her a coat of beaten gold, but still she would not take the old man. She went again to the hen-wife, who said, "Say you will not take him unless he gives you a coat made of the feathers of all the birds of the air." So he sent out a man with a great heap of peas; and the man cried to all birds of the air, "Each bird take a pea and put down a feather." So each bird took a pea and put down one of its feathers. The man took all the feathers and made a coat of them and gave it to her. But still she would not take the nasty, horrid old man. She asked the hen-wife once again what she was to do, and the hen-wife said, "Say he must first make you a coat of fur from wild cats." Then he made her a coat of catskin, and she put it on. Then she tied up her other clothes into a bundle, and when it was dark ran away with it into the woods.

She went along and went along and went along, till at the end of the wood she saw a fine castle. She hid her fine clothes by a crystal waterfall and went up to the castle gates and asked for work. The lady of the castle saw her, and told her, "I'm sorry I have no better job, but if you like you may work in our kitchen." So down she went into the kitchen, and they called her Catskin, because of her coat. But the cook was very cruel to her, and made her life miserable.

Soon after that it happened that the young lord of the castle came home, and there was to be a grand ball in honor of the occasion. When they were speaking about it among the servants, Catskin said, "Dear me, Mrs. Cook, how much I should like to go!"

"What! You impudent girl," said the cook. "How can you go among all the fine lords and ladies with your coat of catskin? A fine figure you'd cut!" And with that she took a basin of water and dashed it over Catskin's head. But Catskin only shook her ears and said nothing.

Now when the day of the ball arrived, Catskin slipped out of the house and went to the edge of the forest where she had hidden her clothes. Then she bathed herself in the crystal waterfall, and put on her coat of silver cloth, and hastened away to the ball. As soon as she entered all were overcome by her beauty and grace, while the young lord at once lost his heart to her. He asked her to be his partner for the first dance, and he would dance with no one else all night long.

When it came time to part, the young lord said, "Pray tell me, fair maid, where do you live?"

But Catskin curtsied and said:

> "Kind sir, if the truth I must tell,
>   At the sign of the 'Basin of Water' I dwell."

Then she flew from the castle and donned her catskin robe again, and slipped into the kitchen, unseen by the cook.

The very next day the young lord went and searched for the sign of the "Basin of Water," but he could not find it. So he went to his mother, the lady of the castle, and declared he would wed no one but the lady of the silver coat, and would never rest till he had found her. So another ball was soon arranged in hopes that the beautiful maid would appear again.

Again Catskin said to the cook, "Oh, how I should like to go!" Whereupon the cook screamed out in a rage, "What! You impudent girl! You would cut a fine figure among all the fine lords and ladies." And with that she banged down her ladle on the stove and broke it. But Catskin only shook her ears, and ran off to the forest, where she bathed and then put on her coat of beaten gold, and off she went to the ballroom.

Catskin

As soon as she entered all eyes were upon her, and the young lord at once recognized her as the lady of the "Basin of Water." He claimed her hand for the first dance, and did not leave her till the last. Again he asked her where she lived. But all that she would say was:

> "Kind sir, if the truth I must tell,
>   At the sign of the 'Broken Ladle' I dwell"

and with that she curtsied and flew from the ball, off with her golden robe, on with her catskin, and into the kitchen without the cook's knowing.

Next day, when the young lord could not find where the sign of the "Broken Ladle" was, he begged his mother to have another grand ball, so that he might meet the beautiful maid once more.

Then Catskin said to the cook, "Oh, how I wish I could go to the ball!" Whereupon the cook called out, "A fine figure you'd cut!" and broke the skimmer across the kettle. But Catskin only shook her ears, and went off to the forest, where she first bathed in the crystal spring, and then donned her coat of feathers, and went off to the ballroom.

When she entered everyone was surprised at so beautiful a face and form dressed in so rich and rare a coat. The young lord at once recognized his beautiful sweetheart, and would dance with no one but her the whole evening. When the ball came to an end he pressed her to tell him where she lived, but all she would answer was:

Catskin

"Kind sir, if the truth I must tell,
   At the sign of the 'Broken Skimmer' I dwell"

and with that she curtsied, and was off to the forest. But this time the young lord followed her, and watched her change her fine coat of feathers for her catskin coat, and then he knew her for his own kitchenmaid.

Next day he went to his mother, and told her that he wished to marry the kitchenmaid, Catskin.

"Never," said the lady of the castle. "Never so long as I live."

The young lord was so grieved that he took to his bed and was very ill indeed. The doctor tried to cure him, but he would not take any medicine unless from the hands of Catskin. At last the doctor went to the mother, and said that her son would die if she did not consent to his marriage with Catskin, so she had to give way. Then she summoned Catskin to her, and Catskin put on her coat of beaten gold before she went to see the lady. The lady was overcome at once, and was only too glad to wed her son to so beautiful a maid.

So they were married, and after a time a little son was born to them, and grew up to be a fine little lad. One day, when he was about four years old, a beggar woman came to the door, and Lady Catskin gave some money to the little boy and told him to give it to the beggar woman. So he went and gave it, putting it into the hand of the woman's baby child. And the child leant forward and kissed the little lord.

Now the wicked old cook (who had never been sent away,

119

because Catskin was too kindhearted) was watching, and she said, "See how beggars' brats take to one another!"

This insult hurt Catskin dreadfully. She went to her husband and told him all about her father, and begged him to go and find out what had become of her parents. So they set out in the lord's grand coach, and traveled through the forest till they came to the house of Catskin's father. While Catskin stayed at a nearby inn, her husband went to see if her father would claim her as his daughter.

Now her father had never had any other child, and his wife had died, so he was all alone in the world and sat moping and miserable. When the young lord came in he hardly looked up, he was so miserable. Catskin's husband drew a chair close up to him, and asked him, "Pray, sir, did you not once have a young daughter whom you would never look at?"

The miserable man said with tears, "It is true; I am a hardened sinner. But I would give all my worldly goods if I could see her once before I die."

Then the young lord told him what had happened to Catskin, and took him to the inn, and afterwards brought his father-in-law to his own castle, where they lived happily ever afterwards.

THE THREE LITTLE PIGS

ONCE upon a time there was an old sow who had three little pigs, and since she did not have enough for them to eat, she said they had better go out into the world and seek their fortunes.

Now the eldest pig went first, and as he trotted along the road he met a man carrying a bundle of straw. So he said very politely, "If you please, sir, could you give me that straw so I might build a house?"

And the man, seeing what good manners the little pig had, gave him the straw, and the little pig set to work and built a beautiful house with it.

When it was finished, a wolf happened to pass that way; and he saw the house, and he smelled the pig inside.

So he knocked at the door and said, *"Little pig! Little pig! Let me in! Let me in!"*

But the little pig saw the wolf's big paws through the keyhole, so he answered back, *"No! No! No! by the hair of my chinny chin chin!"*

Then the wolf showed his teeth and said, *"Then I'll huff and I'll puff and I'll blow your house in."*

So he huffed and he puffed and he blew the house in. Then he ate up the little pig and went on his way.

The Three Little Pigs

Now, the next pig when he started, met a man carrying a bundle of sticks, and, being very polite, he said to him, "If you please, sir, could you give me those sticks so I might build a house?"

And the man, seeing what good manners the little pig had, gave him the sticks and the little pig set to work and built himself a beautiful house.

Now it so happened that when the house was finished the wolf passed that way; and he saw the house, and he smelled the pig inside.

So he knocked at the door and said, *"Little pig! Little pig! Let me in! Let me in!"*

But the little pig peeped through the keyhole and saw the wolf's great ears, so he answered back, *"No! No! No! by the hair of my chinny chin chin!"*

Then the wolf showed his teeth and said, *"Then I'll huff and I'll puff and I'll blow your house in!"*

So he huffed and he puffed and he blew the house in. Then he ate up the little pig and went on his way.

Now the third little pig, when he started, met a man carrying a load of bricks and being very polite, he said, "If you

please, sir, could you give me those bricks so that I might build a house?''

And the man, seeing that he had been well brought up, gave him the bricks, and the little pig set to work and built himself a beautiful house.

And once again when the house was finished the wolf chanced to come that way; and he saw the house, and he smelled the pig inside.

So he knocked at the door and said, *"Little pig! Little pig! Let me in! Let me in!"*

But the little pig peeped through the keyhole and saw the wolf's great eyes, so he answered, *"No! No! No! by the hair of my chinny chin chin!"*

"Then I'll huff and I'll puff and I'll blow your house in!" said the wolf, showing his teeth.

So he huffed and he puffed. He puffed and he huffed. And he huffed, huffed, and he puffed, puffed; but he could *not* blow the house down. At last he was so out of breath that he couldn't huff and he couldn't puff anymore. So he thought a bit. Then he said, "Little pig! I know where there is a nice field of turnips."

"Do you?" said little pig, "And where may that be?"

The Three Little Pigs

"I'll show you." says the wolf, "If you will be ready at six o'clock tomorrow morning, I will call round for you, and we can go together to Farmer Smith's field and get turnips for dinner."

"Thank you kindly," said the little pig. "I will be ready at six o'clock sharp."

But the little pig was not so easily fooled. He got up at five, trotted off to Farmer Smith's field, rooted up the turnips, and was home eating them for breakfast when the wolf clattered at the door and cried, "Little pig! Little pig! Aren't you ready?"

"Ready?" said the little pig. "Why, what a sluggard you are! I've been to the field and come back again, and I'm having a nice potful of turnips for breakfast."

Then the wolf grew red with rage; but he was determined to eat the little pig, so he said, as if he didn't care, "I'm glad you like them, but I know of something better than turnips."

"Oh really?" said the little pig, "And what may that be?"

"A nice apple tree down in Merry Gardens with the juiciest, sweetest apples on it! So if you will be ready at five o'clock tomorrow morning I will come round for you and we can get the apples together."

"Thank you kindly," said the little pig. "I will surely be ready at five o'clock sharp."

The Three Little Pigs

Now the next morning he awoke very early, so it wasn't even four o'clock when he started out to get the apples; but the wolf had been fooled once and wasn't going to be taken in again, so he also started at four o'clock, and the little pig had just gotten his basket half full of apples when he saw the wolf coming down the road licking his lips.

"Hello!" said the wolf, "Here already? You *are* an early bird! Are the apples nice?"

"Very nice," said the little pig. "I'll throw you one to try."

And he threw it so far away, that when the wolf had gone to pick it up, the little pig was able to jump down with his basket and run home.

Well, the wolf was very angry; but he went the next day to the little pig's house and called through the door, as sweet as sugar, "Little pig! Little pig! You are so clever, I should like to take you to the fair tomorrow afternoon."

"Thank you kindly," said the little pig. "What time shall we start?"

"At three o'clock sharp," said the wolf, "so be sure to be ready."

"I'll be ready before three," snickered the little pig. And he was! He started early in the morning and went to the fair, and rode in a swing, and enjoyed himself so much, and bought himself a butter churn and trotted away toward home long before three o'clock. But just as he got to the top of the hill, what should he see but the wolf coming along, panting and red with rage!

Well, there was no place to hide in but the butter churn; so he crept into it, and was just pulling down the cover when the churn started to roll down the hill—

Bumpety, bumpety, bump!

Of course the pig inside began to squeal, and when the wolf heard the noise, and saw the butter churn rolling down on top of him—

Bumpety, bumpety, bump!

—he was so frightened that he turned tail and ran away. But he was still determined to get the little pig for his dinner. So he went next day to the house and told the little pig how sorry he was not to have been able to keep his promise of going to the fair, because of an awful, dreadful, terrible Thing that had rushed at him, making a fearsome noise.

"Dear me!" said the little pig. "That must have been me! I hid inside the butter churn when I saw you coming, and it started to roll! I am sorry I frightened you!"

This was too much for the wolf. He danced about with rage and swore he would come down the chimney and eat the little pig for his supper. But while he was climbing onto the roof the little pig made up a blazing fire and put on a big pot full of water to boil. Then, just as the wolf was coming down the chimney, the little pig took off the lid, and *plump!* the wolf fell into the scalding water.

So the little pig slapped the cover on again, and that was the end of that big, bad wolf!

MR. AND MRS. VINEGAR

MR. AND MRS. VINEGAR lived in a glass pickle jar. The house, though small, was snug, and so light that each speck of dust on the furniture showed up like a molehill. While Mr. Vinegar tilled his garden with a pickle fork and grew vegetables for pickling, Mrs. Vinegar, who was a sharp, bustling, tidy woman, swept, brushed, and dusted, brushed and dusted and swept to keep the house clean as a new pin. One day she lost her temper with a cobweb and swept so hard after it that bang! bang! the broom handle went right through the glass, and crash! crash! clitter! clatter! the pickle jar house fell about her all in splinters and bits.

She picked her way over these as best she might, and rushed into the garden.

"Oh, Vinegar, Vinegar!" she cried. "We are ruined and done for! Stop tending these vegetables! What is the use of pickles if you haven't a pickle jar to put them in! And I've broken ours into little bits!" And with that she fell to crying bitterly.

But Mr. Vinegar, although a small man, was a cheerful one, always looking at the bright side of things. "Accidents will happen, lovey!" he said. "There are other good pickle bottles in the shop. All we need is money to buy another. So let's go out into the world and seek our fortunes."

Mr. and Mrs. Vinegar

"But what about the furniture?" sobbed Mrs. Vinegar.

"I will take the door of the house with me, lovey," said Mr. Vinegar stoutly. "Then no one will be able to open it, will they?"

Mrs. Vinegar did not quite see how this fact would mend matters but she held her peace. And off they trudged into the world to seek their fortune, Mr. Vinegar bearing the door on his back like a snail carries its house.

They walked all day long, but not a penny did they make, and when night fell they found themselves in a dark, thick forest. Now Mrs. Vinegar, even though she was a smart, strong woman, was tired to death, and afraid of wild beasts, so she began to cry bitterly; but Mr. Vinegar was as cheerful as ever.

"Don't alarm yourself, lovey," he said. "I will climb into a tree, fix the door firmly in a fork, and you can sleep there as safe and comfortable as in your own bed."

So he climbed the tree, fixed the door, and Mrs. Vinegar lay down on it, and being dead tired was soon fast asleep. But her weight tilted the door sideways and, after a time, Mr. Vinegar, afraid she might slip off, sat down on the other side to balance her and keep watch.

In the middle of the night, just as he was beginning to nod, what should happen but that a band of robbers met beneath that very tree to divide their spoils. Mr. Vinegar could hear every word they said, and began to tremble like an aspen leaf as he listened to the terrible deeds the thieves had done.

"Don't shake so!" murmured Mrs. Vinegar, half asleep. "You'll roll me off the bed."

Mr. and Mrs. Vinegar

"I'm not shaking, lovey," whispered back Mr. Vinegar in a quaking voice. "It is only the wind in the trees."

But for all his cheerfulness he was not really *very* brave *inside,* so he went on trembling and shaking, and shaking and trembling, until, just as the robbers were beginning to divide the money, he actually shook the door right out of the tree-fork, and down it came—with Mrs. Vinegar still asleep upon it —right on top of the robbers' heads!

As you may imagine, they thought the sky had fallen, and ran away as fast as their legs would carry them, leaving their booty behind them. Mr. Vinegar, who had saved himself from the fall by clinging to a branch, was far too frightened to go down in the dark to see what had happened. So up in the tree he sat like a big bird until dawn came.

Then Mrs. Vinegar woke, rubbed her eyes, yawned, and said, "Where am I?"

"On the ground, lovey," answered Mr. Vinegar, scrambling down.

And when they lifted up the door, what do you think they found?

One robber squashed flat as a pancake, and forty golden coins all scattered about!

My goodness! How Mr. and Mrs. Vinegar jumped for joy!

"Now, Vinegar!" said his wife when they had gathered up all the gold pieces, "I will tell you what we must do. You must go to the next town and buy a cow. A cow will give us milk and butter, which we can sell, and we shall live in comfort for the rest of our days."

Mr. and Mrs. Vinegar

"How smart you are, lovey!" said Mr. Vinegar admiringly, and started off on his errand.

"Remember, make a good bargain," called his wife after him.

"I always do," called back Mr. Vinegar. "I made a good bargain when I married such a clever wife, and I made a better one when I shook her down from the tree. I am the happiest man alive!"

So he trudged on, laughing and jingling the forty gold pieces in his pocket.

The first thing he saw in the market was an old red cow. "I am in luck today," he thought. "That is the very cow for me. I shall be the happiest of men if I get that cow." So he went up to the owner, jingling the gold in his pocket.

"How much do you want for your cow?" he asked.

And the owner of the cow, seeing that Mr. Vinegar was a simpleton, said, "Whatever you've got in your pocket."

"Done!" said Mr. Vinegar. He handed over the forty gold pieces and led off the cow, marching her up and down the market, much against her will, to show off his bargain.

As he drove the cow about, proud and happy, he noticed a man who was playing the bagpipes. He was followed about by a crowd of children who danced to the music, and a shower of pennies fell into his cap every time he held it out.

"Ho, ho!" thought Mr. Vinegar. "That is an easier way of earning a livelihood than by driving about a cow! Think of the feeding, and the milking, and the churning! Ah, I should be the happiest man alive if I had those bagpipes!"

Mr. and Mrs. Vinegar

So he went up to the musician and said, "What will you take for your bagpipes?"

"Well," replied the musician, seeing he was a simpleton, "it is a beautiful instrument, and I make so much money by it, that I cannot take anything less than that red cow."

"Done!" cried Mr. Vinegar in a hurry, before the man could change his mind.

So the musician walked off with the red cow, and Mr. Vinegar tried to play the bagpipes. But, alas and alack! though he blew till he almost burst, not a sound could he make at first. When he did at last produce a sound, it was such a terrific squeal and screech that all the children ran away frightened, and the people put their fingers in their ears.

But he went on and on, trying to play a tune, and never earning anything, until his fingers were almost frozen with the cold; then, of course, the noise he made on the bagpipes was worse than ever.

Then he noticed a man who had on a pair of warm gloves, and he said to himself, "Music is impossible when one's fingers are frozen. I believe I should be the happiest man alive if I had those gloves."

So he went up to the owner and said, "You seem, sir, to have a very good pair of gloves." And the man replied, "Truly, sir, my hands are as warm as toast on this bitterly cold November day."

Mr. Vinegar asked at once how much the owner wanted for them. The owner, seeing he was a simpleton, said, "As your hands seem frozen, sir, I will, as a favor, let you have them for your bagpipes."

Mr. and Mrs. Vinegar

"Done!" cried Mr. Vinegar, delighted, and made the exchange.

Then he set off to find his wife, quite pleased with himself. "Warm hands, warm heart!" he thought. "I'm the happiest man alive!"

But as he trudged he grew very, very tired, and at last began to limp. Then he saw a man coming along the road with a stout stick.

"I should be the happiest man alive if I had that stick," he thought. "What is the use of warm hands if your feet ache!" So he said to the man with the stick, "What will you take for your stick?" And the man, seeing he was a simpleton, replied, "Well, I don't want to part with my stick, but as you are eager I'll oblige you, as a friend, in exchange for those warm gloves you are wearing."

"Done!" cried Mr. Vinegar delightedly, and trudged off with the stick, chuckling to himself over his good bargain.

But as he went along a magpie fluttered out of the hedge and sat on a branch in front of him, and laughed as magpies do. "What are you laughing at?" asked Mr. Vinegar.

"At you!" chuckled the magpie, fluttering away just a little further. "At *you*, Mr. Vinegar, you foolish man—you blockhead! You bought a cow for forty gold pieces when she wasn't worth ten, you exchanged her for bagpipes you couldn't play, you changed the bagpipes for a pair of gloves, and the pair of gloves for a miserable stick. Ho, ho! Ha, ha! So you've nothing to show for your forty gold pieces but a stick you might have cut from any hedge. Ah, you fool! You simpleton! You blockhead!"

Mr. and Mrs. Vinegar

And the magpie chuckled and chuckled and chuckled in big guffaws, fluttering from branch to branch as Mr. Vinegar trudged along, until at last he flung his stick at the bird. And the stick stuck in a tree out of his reach; so he had to go back to his wife without anything at all.

Mr. and Mrs. Vinegar

But he was glad the stick had stuck in a tree, for Mrs. Vinegar's hands were quite hard enough without a stick in them, and she thwacked him until he was silly.

Mr. Vinegar said cheerfully, "You are too violent, lovey. You broke the pickle jar, and now you've nearly broken every bone in my body. I think we had better turn over a new leaf and begin anew. I shall take a job as a gardener, and you can be a housemaid, until we have enough money to buy a new pickle jar." And that is the story of Mr. and Mrs. Vinegar.

THE TRUE HISTORY OF
SIR THOMAS THUMB

AT the court of the great King Arthur, who lived when knights were bold and ladies were fair, one of the most famous men was the wizard Merlin. Never before or since was there such a one as he. All that was to be known about wizardry he knew, and his advice was always good and kind.

Once when he was traveling disguised as a beggar, he came upon an honest plowman and his wife who gave him a hearty welcome and supplied him, cheerfully, with a big wooden bowl of fresh milk and some coarse brown bread on a wooden platter. Although they and the little cottage where they lived were neat and tidy, Merlin noticed that neither the husband nor the wife seemed happy; and when he asked why they said it was because they had no children.

"Had I a son, even if he were no bigger than my good man's thumb," said the poor woman, "we should be quite content."

The idea of a boy no bigger than a man's thumb so tickled Wizard Merlin's fancy that he promised straight away that such a son should come in due time to bring the good couple happiness. This said, he went off at once to pay a visit to the Queen of the Fairies, since he felt that the little people would best be able to carry out his promise. And, sure enough, the fancy of a boy no bigger than his father's thumb tickled the Fairy Queen also, and she set about the task at once.

The plowman and his wife were as happy as a king and queen over the tiniest of tiny babies, and even happier because the Fairy Queen, anxious to see the little fellow, flew in the window, bringing clothes fit for the tiny boy to wear.

An oak leaf hat he had for his crown;
His jacket was woven of thistle down.
His shirt was a web by spiders spun;
His breeches of softest feathers were done.
His stockings of red apple skin were sewn
With an eyelash plucked from his mother's own.
His shoes were made of a mouse's hide
Tanned with the soft furry hair inside.

All dressed up he was the prettiest little fellow ever seen, and the Fairy Queen kissed him over and over again, and gave him the name of Tom Thumb.

Now as he grew older—although, mind you, he never grew bigger—he was so full of antics and tricks that he was forever getting into trouble. Once his mother was making a batter pudding, and Tom, wanting to see how it was made, climbed up to the edge of the bowl. His mother was so busy beating the batter that she didn't notice him; and when his foot slipped and he tumbled head over heels into the bowl, she just went on beating until the batter was light enough. Then she tied it up into the pudding cloth and set it over a steaming kettle fire to cook.

Now the batter had so filled poor Tom's mouth that he couldn't cry; but no sooner did he feel the hot water than he began to struggle and kick so much that the pudding bobbed up and down in such strange fashion that the plowman's wife thought it was bewitched, and in a great fright flung the pudding out the door.

A poor tinker passing by picked it up and put it in his pocket. By this time Tom had got his mouth clear of the batter, and he began hollering, and making such a noise, that the tinker, even more frightened than Tom's mother had been, threw the pudding in the road, and ran away as fast as he could. Luckily for Tom, this second fall broke the string holding the pudding-cloth and he was able to creep out, all covered with half-cooked batter, and make his way home. His mother, distressed to see her little dear in such a woeful state, put him into a teacup full of water to wash him, and then tucked him into bed.

Another time Tom's mother went to milk her red cow in the meadow and took Tom with her, for she was always afraid that he might get into mischief if left alone. The wind was high, and worried that he would be blown away, she tied him to the top of a thistle with one of her own long hairs, and then began to milk. But the red cow, nosing about for something to do while she was being milked, spied Tom's oak-leaf hat and, thinking it looked good, curled its tongue round the thistle stalk and——

The True History of Sir Thomas Thumb

There was Tom dodging the cow's teeth and roaring as loud as he could, "Mother! Mother! Help! Help!"

"Laws-a-mercy-me!" cried his mother. "Where's the child got to now? Where are you, you bad boy?"

"Here!" roared Tom, "in the red cow's mouth!"

With that his mother began to weep and wail, not knowing what else to do. Tom, hearing her, roared louder than ever. At that, the red cow, alarmed—and no wonder—at the dreadful noise coming from her throat, opened her mouth, and Tom dropped out, luckily into his mother's apron.

Adventures like these were not Tom's fault because he could not help being so small. But once he got into dreadful trouble for which he was entirely to blame. This is what happened. He loved tossing cherry pits with the big boys, and when he had lost all his own he would creep into the other players' bags and make off with enough cherry pits to carry on the game!

One day one of the boys saw Master Tom on the point of coming out of a bag with a whole fistful of cherry pits. So he just drew the string of the bag tight.

"Ha ha! Mr. Thomas Thumb," he said jeeringly. "So you were going to steal my cherry pits, were you? Well! You shall have more of them than you like." And with that he gave the bag of cherry pits such a hearty shake that all Tom's body and legs were bruised black and blue and he wasn't let out till he had promised never to steal cherry pits again.

The years passed, and when Tom was a lad, still no bigger than a thumb, his father thought he might begin to make himself useful. He made him a whip out of a straw, and set him

The True History of Sir Thomas Thumb

to drive the cattle home. But Tom, in trying to climb a fur-row's ridge—which to him, of course, was a steep hill—slipped down and lay half stunned. A raven flying over thought he was a frog, and picked him up intending to eat him. Not liking the taste of the morsel, however, the bird dropped him above the battlements of a big castle that stood close to the sea. Now the castle belonged to Grumbo, an ill-tempered giant who happened to be walking on the roof of his tower. And when Tom dropped onto his bald head the giant put up his great hand to catch what he thought was an impudent fly. Finding something that smelled like meat, he just swallowed the little fellow as he would have swallowed a pill!

However, he soon began to regret it, for Tom kicked and struggled in the giant's inside as he had done in the red cow's throat until the giant felt quite squeamish, and finally spit Tom out over the battlements and into the sea.

And here would have been Tom Thumb's end by drown-ing, had not a big fish, thinking that he was a shrimp, rushed up and gulped him down!

Luckily some fishermen were nearby and when they drew in their nets the fish that had swallowed Tom was one of the haul. Being a very fine fish it was sent to the Court kitchen; when the fish was opened, out popped Tom onto the table, as spry as spry could be, to the astonishment of the cook! Never had such a tiny man been seen, and his quips and pranks kept the whole pantry in roars of laughter. He soon became the favorite of the whole Court, and when the King went out riding Tom sat in the pocket of his vest ready to amuse royalty and the Knights of the Round Table.

The True History of Sir Thomas Thumb

After a while, however, Tom longed to see his parents again; so the King gave him permission to go home and take with him as much money as he could carry. Tom chose a threepenny piece, and putting it into a purse made of a water bubble, lifted it with difficulty on to his back, and trudged away to his father's house, which was some half a mile away.

It took him two days and two nights to cover the ground, and he was wearied by his heavy burden before he reached home. His mother put him to bed in a walnut shell by the fire and gave him a whole hazel nut to eat, which made him sick for a whole nut usually lasted him a month. He recovered in time, but had grown so thin and light that to save him the trouble of walking back to the Court, his mother tied him to a dandelion puff, and away he went on a high wind, as if on wings. Unfortunately, just as he was flying low in order to alight, the Court cook, an ill-natured fellow, was coming across the palace yard with a bowl of hot porridge and cream for the King's supper. Now Tom was unskilled in the handling of dandelion puffs, so he rode straight into the porridge, spilled half of it, and splashed the other half, scalding hot, into the cook's face.

He was in a fine rage, and going straight to King Arthur said that Tom, at his old antics, had done it on purpose.

Now the King's favorite dish was hot porridge and cream; so he also fell into a fine rage and ordered Tom to be tried for high treason. He was imprisoned in a mousetrap, where he remained for several days tormented by a cat who, thinking him some new kind of mouse, spent its time poking at him through the bars. At the end of a week, however, King Arthur sent for Tom and once more received him into favor. After this Tom's life was happy and successful. He became so renowned for his dexterity and cleverness, that he was knighted by the King under the name of Sir Thomas Thumb. As his clothes— what with the batter and the hot porridge, to say nothing of the insides of giants and fishes—had become somewhat shabby, the King ordered him a new suit of clothes fit for a knight to wear. He also gave him a beautiful prancing gray mouse as a charger.

It was certainly diverting to see Tom dressed up to the nines, and as proud as he could be.

Of butterflies' wings his shirt was made,
His boots of chicken hide,
And by a nimble fairy blade,
All learned in the tailoring trade,
His coat was well supplied.
A needle dangled at his side,
And thus attired in stately pride
A dapper mouse he used to ride.

In truth the King and all the Knights of the Round Table were ready to expire with laughter at Tom on his fine dancing steed.

But one day, as the hunt was passing a farmhouse, a big cat, lurking about, made one spring and carried both Tom and the mouse up a tree. Undaunted, Tom boldly drew his needle sword and attacked the enemy with such fierceness that she let her prey fall. Luckily one of the nobles caught the little fellow in his cap, otherwise he would have been killed by the fall. As it was he became very ill, and the doctor despaired of his life. However, his friend and guardian, the Queen of the Fairies, arrived in a chariot drawn by flying mice, and then and there carried Tom back with her to Fairyland, where, among folk of his own size, he was able to recover. But time runs swiftly in Fairyland, and when Tom Thumb returned to Court he was surprised to find that his father and mother and nearly all his old friends were dead, and that King Thunstone reigned in King Arthur's place. Everyone was astonished at his size, and carried him as a curiosity to the Audience Hall.

"Who are you, little man?" asked King Thunstone. "Where do you come from? And where do you live?"

To which Tom replied with a bow:

"My name is well known.
From the Fairies I come.
When King Arthur shone,
This Court was my home.
By him I was knighted,
In me he delighted
Your servant—Sir Thomas Thumb."

This address so pleased the King that he ordered a little golden chair to be made, so that Tom might sit beside him at the dinner table; as well as a little palace of gold, no higher than your hand, with doors a bare inch wide, in which the little fellow might sleep at night.

The True History of Sir Thomas Thumb

Now King Thunstone's Queen was a very jealous woman, and could not bear to see such honors showered on the little fellow; so she told the King all sorts of bad tales about his favorite, saying that he had been saucy and rude to her.

The King sent for Tom. But knowing by bitter experience the danger of royal displeasure, Tom hid himself in an empty snailshell, where he lay till he was nearly starved. Then seeing a fine large butterfly on a dandelion close by, he climbed up and managed to get astride it. No sooner had he gained his seat than the butterfly was off, hovering from tree to tree, from flower to flower.

At last the royal gardener saw it and gave chase. Then the nobles joined in the hunt, even the King himself, and finally the Queen, who forgot her anger in the merriment. Hither and thither they ran, trying in vain to catch the pair, and almost expiring with laughter, until poor Tom, dizzy with so much fluttering and flittering, fell from his seat into a watering pot, where he nearly drowned.

So they all agreed he must be forgiven, because he had afforded them so much amusement.

Thus Tom was once more in favor; but he did not live long to enjoy his good luck, for one day a spider attacked him. Though he fought well, the creature's poisonous breath proved too much for him and he fell dead on the ground where he stood.

Thus ended Sir Thomas Thumb; but the King and the Court were so sorry at the loss of their little favorite that they went into mourning for him. And they put a fine white marble

monument over his grave on which was carved the following
epitaph:

> Here lies Tom Thumb, King Arthur's Knight,
> Who died by a spider's cruel bite.
> He was well known in Arthur's Court,
> Where he afforded gallant sport.
> He rode at tilt and tournament,
> And on a mouse a-hunting went.
> Alive he filled the Court with mirth,
> His death to sadness must give birth.
> So wipe your eyes and shake your head,
> And say, "Alas, Tom Thumb is dead!"

They thanked her for her kindness and said good-bye
Page 148

"Well!" she chuckled, "I am in luck!"
Page 170

THE THREE HEADS OF THE WELL

ONCE upon a time there reigned a King in Colchester, valiant, strong, wise, and famous as a good ruler.

But in the midst of his glory his dear Queen died, leaving him with a daughter renowned far and wide for her beauty, kindness, and grace. Now strange things happen, and the King of Colchester, hearing of a lady who had immense riches, decided to marry her although she was old, ugly, hooknosed, and ill-tempered; furthermore, she had a daughter as ugly as herself. No one could give the reason why, but only a few weeks after the death of his dear Queen, the King brought this loathsome bride to Court, and married her with great pomp and festivities. Now the very first thing she did was to poison the King's mind against his own beautiful daughter, of whom, naturally, the ugly Queen and her ugly daughter were dreadfully jealous.

When the young Princess found that her father had turned against her, she grew weary of Court life, and longed to get away from it. One day, happening to meet the King alone in the garden, she went down on her knees, and begged him to let her go out into the world to seek her fortune. The King agreed, and told his Queen to fit the girl out for her enterprise in proper fashion. But the jealous woman only gave her a canvas bag of brown bread and hard cheese, and a bottle of cider.

Although this was a pitiful dowry for a king's daughter, the Princess was too proud to complain. She gave her thanks, and set off on her journey through woods and forests, by rivers and lakes, over mountain and valley.

At last she came to a cave at the mouth of which, on a stone, sat an old, old man with a white beard.

"Good morning, fair damsel," he said. "Where are you going?"

"Old gentleman," she replied, "I go to seek my fortune."

"And what do you have in your bag and bottle for dowry, fair damsel?" he asked.

"Bread and cheese and cider, sir," said she, smiling. "Will it please you to share it with me?"

"With all my heart," said he, and when she pulled out her provisions he ate nearly all of them. But once again she made no complaint, and told him to eat what he needed.

Now when he had finished he gave her many thanks, and said, "For your kindness and your grace, take this wand. There is a thick thorny hedge before you which seems impassable. But strike it three times with this wand, saying each time, 'Please, hedge, let me through,' and it will open a pathway for you. Then, when you come to a well, sit down on the brink of it; do not be surprised at anything you may see or hear, but do whatever you are asked to do."

Then the old man went into the cave, and the maiden went on her way. After a while she came to a high, thick thorny hedge. When she struck it three times with the wand, saying, "Please, hedge, let me through," it opened a wide pathway for her. So she came to the well, on the brink of which she sat down. No sooner was she seated, than a golden head without any body came up through the water, singing as it came:

> "Wash me, and comb me, lay me on a bank to dry
>   Softly and prettily to watch the passersby."

"Certainly," she said, pulling out her silver comb. Then, placing the head on her lap, she began to comb the golden hair. When she had combed it, she lifted the golden head softly, and laid it on a primrose bank to dry. No sooner had she done this than another golden head appeared, singing as it came:

> "Wash me, and comb me, lay me on a bank to dry
>   Softly and prettily to watch the passersby."

"Certainly," she said, and after combing the golden hair, placed the golden head softly on the primrose bank, beside the first one.

Then came a third head out of the well, and it said the same thing:

> "Wash me, and comb me, lay me on a bank to dry
>   Softly and prettily to watch the passersby."

"With all my heart," said she graciously, and after taking the head on her lap, and combing its golden hair with her silver comb, there were the three golden heads in a row on the primrose bank. And she sat down to rest herself and looked at them, they were so quaint and pretty. As she rested she cheerfully ate and drank the meager portion of the brown bread, hard cheese, and cider which the old man had left to her, for, although she was a king's daughter, she was too proud to complain.

Then the first head spoke. "Brothers, what shall we wish for this damsel who has been so gracious to us? I wish her to be so beautiful that she shall charm everyone she meets."

"And I," said the second head, "wish her a voice sweeter than the nightingale's."

"And I," said the third head, "wish her to be so fortunate that she shall marry the greatest king that reigns."

"Thank you with all my heart," said she, "but don't you think I had better put you back in the well before I go on? Remember you are golden, and the passersby might steal you."

To this they agreed, so she put them back. And when they had thanked her for her kindness and said good-bye, she went on her journey.

She had not traveled far before she came to a forest where the King of that country was hunting with his nobles, and as the cavalcade passed down the glade she stood back to avoid them; but the King caught sight of her and drew up his horse.

"Fair maid," he said, "who are you, and where are you going through the forest all alone?"

"I am the King of Colchester's daughter, and I go to seek

my fortune," said she, and her voice was sweeter than the nightingale's.

Then the King jumped down from his horse, being so struck by her beauty that he felt he couldn't live without her, and falling on one knee begged her to marry him without delay.

And he begged and prayed so well that at last she consented. With all courtesy, he mounted her behind him on his horse and, commanding the hunt to follow, he returned to his palace, where the wedding festivities took place with all possible pomp and merriment. Then, ordering out the royal chariot, the happy pair started to pay the King of Colchester a bridal visit. You may imagine the surprise and delight with which, after so short an absence, the people of Colchester saw their beloved Princess return in a chariot all trimmed with gold as the bride of the most powerful King in the world. The bells rang out, flags flew, drums beat, and the people cheered. Everyone was happy except for the ugly Queen and her ugly daughter, who were ready to burst with envy and malice.

After the visit was ended, and the young King and his bride had gone back to their own country to live happily ever after, the ugly ill-natured Princess said to her mother, the ugly Queen, "I also will go into the world and seek my fortune. If that drab of a girl with her mincing ways got so much, I should do even better."

So her mother agreed, and furnished her with silken dresses and furs, and gave her provisions of sugar, almonds, and sweetmeats of every variety, along with a large bottle of excellent wine—altogether a right royal dowry.

Armed with these she set forth, following the same road as her stepsister. She soon came upon the old man with a white beard, who was seated on a stone by the mouth of a cave.

"Good morning," said he. "Where are you going?"

"What's that to you, old man?" she replied rudely.

"And what do you have for dowry in your bag and bottle?" he asked quietly.

"Good things with which you shall not be troubled," she answered pertly.

"Can you spare an old man something?" he asked.

Then she laughed. "Not a bite, not a sip, for they might choke you, although that would be small matter to me," she replied, with a toss of her head.

"Then ill luck go with you," remarked the old man as he rose and went into the cave.

So she went on her way, and after a time came to the thick thorny hedge, and seeing what she thought was a gap in it, she tried to pass through; but no sooner had she got well into the middle of the hedge than the thorns closed in around her so that she was all scratched and torn before she worked her way out. Streaming with blood, she went on to the well and sat on the brink intending to cleanse herself. But just as she dipped her hands into the water, up came a golden head singing as it came,

"Wash me, and comb me, lay me on the bank to dry
    Softly and prettily to watch the passersby."

150

The Three Heads of the Well

"A likely story," said she. "I'm going to wash myself." And with that she gave the head such a bang with her bottle that it bobbed below the water. But it came up again, and so did a second head, singing as it came:

"Wash me, and comb me, lay me on the bank to dry
  Softly and prettily to watch the passersby."

"Not I," scoffed she. "I'm going to wash *my* hands and face and have my dinner." And she gave the second head a cruel bang with the bottle, and both heads ducked down in the water.

But when they came up again all draggled and dripping, the third head came also, singing as it came:

The Three Heads of the Well

"Wash me, and comb me, lay me on the bank to dry
Softly and prettily to watch the passersby."

By this time the ugly Princess had cleansed herself and, seated on the primrose bank, had her mouth full of sugar and almonds.

"Not I," said she as well as she could. "I'm not a washerwoman nor a barber. So take that for your washing and combing."

And with that, having finished the bottle of wine, she flung the empty bottle at the three heads.

But this time they didn't duck. They looked at each other and said, "What shall we wish this rude girl for her bad manners?"

Then the first head said, "I wish that to her ugliness shall be added blotches on her face."

And the second head said, "I wish that she shall ever be hoarse as a crow and speak as if she had her mouth full."

Then the third head said, "And I wish that she shall be glad to marry a shoemaker."

Then the three heads sank into the well and were no more seen, and the ugly Princess went on her way. But, lo and behold! when she came to a town, the children ran from her ugly blotched face screaming with fright, and when she tried to tell them she was the King of Colchester's daughter, her voice squeaked and was hoarse as a crow's, and folk could not understand a word she said, because she spoke as if her mouth was full!

Now in the town there happened to be a cobbler who not

long before had mended the shoes of a poor old hermit. The hermit had no money and had paid for the job with the gift of a wonderful ointment which would cure blotches on the face, and a bottle of medicine that would banish any hoarseness.

Seeing the miserable, ugly Princess in great distress, the shoemaker went up to her and gave her a few drops out of his bottle. Seeing from her rich attire and clearer speech that she was indeed a King's daughter, he craftily said that if she would take him for a husband he would cure her.

"Anything! Anything!" sobbed the miserable Princess.

So they were married, and the cobbler set off with his bride to visit the King of Colchester. But the bells did not ring, the drums did not beat, and the people, instead of cheering, burst into loud guffaws at the cobbler in leather, and his wife in silks and satins.

As for the ugly Queen, she was so enraged and disappointed that she went mad and ran off in a temper. The King, really pleased at getting rid of her so soon, gave the cobbler a hundred pounds and told him go about his business with his ugly bride.

Which he did quite happily, for a hundred pounds means a great deal to a poor cobbler. Oh, yes the cobbler gave his bride the wonderful ointment which cured her splotches and a few more drops from his bottle of medicine completely banished her hoarseness. They went to a remote part of the kingdom and lived for many years, he mending shoes, and she spinning the thread for him.

DICK WHITTINGTON AND HIS CAT

MORE than five hundred years ago there was a little boy named Dick Whittington, and this is true. His father and mother died when he was too young to work, and so poor little Dick was very badly off. He was quite glad to get the parings of the potatoes to eat and a dry crust of bread now and then, and more than that he did not often get, for the village where he lived was a very poor one and the neighbors were not able to spare him much.

Now the country folk in those days thought that the people of London were all fine ladies and gentlemen, and that there was singing and dancing all the day long, and so rich were they there that even the streets, they said, were paved with gold. Dick used to sit and listen while all these strange tales of the wealth of London were told, and it made him long to go and live there and have plenty to eat and fine clothes to wear, instead of the rags and poor food that were his lot in the country.

So one day when a great wagon with eight horses stopped on its way through the village, Dick made friends with the wagon driver and begged for a ride to London. The man felt sorry for poor little Dick when he heard that he had no father or mother to take care of him, and saw how ragged and how

155

badly in need of help he was. So he agreed to take him, and off they set.

How far it was and how many days they took over the journey I do not know, but in due time Dick found himself in the wonderful city in which he had pictured himself so grandly. But oh! How disappointed he was when he got there. How dirty it was! And the people were so unlike the lively company with music and singing that he had dreamed of! He wandered up and down the streets, one after another, until he was tired out, but he did not find one street that was paved with gold. Dirt in plenty he could see, but none of the gold that he expected to put in his pockets as fast as he picked it up.

Little Dick ran about till he was tired and it was growing dark. And at last he sat down in a corner and fell asleep. When morning came he was very cold and hungry, and though he asked everyone he met to help him, only one or two gave him a halfpenny to buy some bread. For two or three days he lived in the streets in this way, only just able to keep himself alive. Then he managed to get some work to do in a hayfield, and that kept him for a short time longer, till the haymaking was over.

After this he was as badly off as ever, and didn't know

where to turn. One day in his wanderings he lay down to rest in the doorway of the house of a rich merchant whose name was Fitzwarren. But here he was soon seen by the cook, who was an unkind, bad-tempered woman. "Lazy rogue," she called him, and threatened to throw some dirty dishwater over him if he didn't go. However, just then Mr. Fitzwarren himself came home to dinner and asked Dick why he was lying there. "You're old enough to be at work, my boy," he said. "I'm afraid you are inclined to be lazy."

"Indeed, sir," said Dick to him, "that is not so." And Dick told him how hard he had tried to get work to do, and how ill he was for lack of food. Dick, poor fellow, was now so weak that although he tried to stand he had to lie down again, for it was more than three days since he had had anything to eat at all. The kind merchant took him into the house and gave him a good dinner, and then he said that he was to do what work he could to help the cook.

Now Dick would have been happy enough in this good family if it had not been for the ill-natured cook, who did her best to make life a burden to him. Night and morning she was forever scolding him. Nothing he did was good enough. It was "Look sharp here" and "Hurry up there," and there was no pleasing her. And many's the swats he had from the broomstick or the ladle, or whatever else she had in her hand.

At last Miss Alice, Mr. Fitzwarren's daughter, learned how badly the cook was treating poor Dick. She told the cook that she would quickly lose her job if she didn't treat him more kindly, for Dick had become quite a favorite with the family.

After that the cook's behavior was a little better, but Dick still had another hardship to bear. He slept in an attic where were so many holes in the walls and the floor, that every night as he lay in bed the room was overrun with rats and mice, and sometimes he could hardly sleep a wink. One day when he had earned a penny for cleaning a gentleman's shoes, he met a little girl with a cat in her arms, and asked whether she would not sell it to him. "Yes, I would," she said, although the cat was such a good mouser that she was sorry to part with her. This just suited Dick, who kept the cat up in his attic, feeding her on scraps of his own dinner that he saved for her every day. In a little while he had no more bother with the rats and mice. The cat soon saw to that, and he slept soundly every night.

Soon after this Mr. Fitzwarren had a ship ready to sail and, as it was his custom that all his servants should be given a chance of good fortune, he called them all into the counting house and asked them what they would ship out to sell in a foreign country.

They all had something that they were willing to try except poor Dick, who had nothing to send. Miss Alice guessed what was the matter, and said, "I will lay down some money for him out of my own purse." But her father told her that would not do, for it must be something of his own.

When Dick heard this he said, "I have nothing whatever but a cat, which I bought for a penny some time ago."

"Go, my boy, fetch your cat then," said his master, "and let her go."

Dick went upstairs and fetched the poor cat, but there were tears in his eyes when he gave her to the captain. "For," he said, "I shall now be kept awake all night by the rats and mice."

Dick Whittington and His Cat

All the company laughed at Dick's odd venture, except Miss Alice, who felt sorry for him.

Now this, and other marks of kindness shown him by Miss Alice, made the ill-tempered cook jealous of poor Dick, and she began to treat him more cruelly than ever, and was always making fun of him for sending his cat to sea. "What do you think your cat will sell for?" she'd ask. "As much money as would buy a stick to beat you with?"

At last poor Dick could not bear it any longer, and decided to run away. He made a bundle of his things and started very early in the morning, on the first of November. He walked as far as Holloway, and there he sat down to rest on a stone, which to this day is called "Whittington's Stone," and began to wonder to himself which road he should take.

Dick Whittington and His Cat

While he was thinking what he should do the bells of Bow Church began to chime, and as they rang he fancied that they were singing over and over again:

> "Turn again, Whittington,
> Lord Mayor of London."

"Lord Mayor of London!" said he to himself. "Why, to be sure, I would put up with almost anything to be Lord Mayor of London, and ride in a fine coach when I grow to be a man! I'll go back, and think nothing of the cuffing and scolding of the cross old cook if I am to be Lord Mayor of London one day."

Back he went, and he was lucky enough to get into the house and set about his work before the cook came down.

But now you must hear what befell Dick's cat all this while. The ship *Unicorn* that she was on was a long time at sea, and the cat made herself useful among the unwelcome rats that lived on board, too. At last the ship put into harbor on the coast of Barbary, where the people had never before seen a ship from England, and flocked in numbers to see the sailors, whose different color and foreign dress were a great wonder to them. They were soon eager to buy the goods with which the ship was laden, and samples were sent ashore for the Barbary king to see. He was so pleased with them that he sent for the captain to come to the palace, and honored him with an invitation to dinner. No sooner were they seated, as is the custom there, on the fine rugs and carpets that covered the floor, than great numbers of rats and mice came scampering in, swarming over all the dishes, and helping themselves from all the good things there were to eat. The captain was amazed, and asked the king's servants if they didn't find such a pest most unpleasant.

"Oh yes," they said, "and the king would give half his treasure to be freed of them, for they not only spoil his dinner, but they even disturb him in his bed at night, so that for fear of them a watch has to be kept while he is sleeping."

The captain was overjoyed; he thought at once of poor Dick Whittington and his cat, and said he had a creature on board ship that would soon kill all these vermin if she were there. When the king heard this he was eager to possess this wonderful animal.

"Bring it to me at once," he said, "for the vermin are dreadful, and if it will do what you say, I will load your ship with gold and jewels in exchange for it."

The captain, who knew his business, took care not to underrate the value of Dick's cat. He told the king how inconvenient it would be to part with her, as when she was gone the rats might destroy the goods in the ship. However, he said, to oblige the king, he would fetch her.

"Oh, run quickly!" cried the queen. "I, too, am eager to see this dear creature."

Off went the captain, while another dinner was got ready. He took the cat under his arm and got back to the palace just in time to see the carpet covered with rats and mice once again. When the cat saw them, she didn't wait to be told, but jumped out of the captain's arms, and in no time almost all the rats and mice were dead at her feet, while the rest of them had scuttled off to their holes in fright.

Dick Whittington and His Cat

The king was delighted to get rid so easily of such an intolerable plague, and the queen asked that the animal who had done them such a service be brought to her. Upon which the captain called out, "Puss, puss, puss," and she came running to him. Then he presented her to the queen, who was afraid at first to touch a creature that was able to kill so many rats and mice. However, when the captain called her, "Pussy, pussy," and began to stroke her, the queen also ventured to touch her and cried, "Putty, putty," in imitation of the captain, for she couldn't speak English. The captain put the cat on the queen's lap, where she purred and played with the lady's hand and soon purred herself to sleep.

When the king saw what the cat could do, and learning that her kittens would soon stock the whole country and keep it free from rats, he bought the whole ship's cargo, and then gave the captain ten times as much for the cat.

The captain then said farewell to the court of Barbary, and after a fair voyage reached London again with his precious load of gold and jewels, safe and sound.

One morning Mr. Fitzwarren had just come to his counting house and settled himself at the desk to count the cash, when there came a knock at the door. "Who's there?" said he. "A friend," replied a voice. "I come with good news of your ship the *Unicorn*." The merchant opened the door, and there stood the ship's captain and the mate, bearing a chest of jewels and gold. When he had looked this over he lifted his eyes and thanked heaven for sending him such a prosperous voyage.

The honest captain next told him all about the cat, and showed him the rich present the king had sent to Dick for her purchase price. Rejoicing on behalf of Dick as much as he had done over his own good fortune, he called out to his servants:

"Go fetch him, and we'll tell him of his fame;
Pray call him Mr. Whittington by name."

Some of the servants hesitated and said so great a treasure was too much for a lad like Dick. But Mr. Fitzwarren now showed himself to be a really good man and refused to deprive him of the value of a single penny. "God forbid!" he cried. "It all belongs to him, and he shall have it, every single penny."

He then sent for Dick, who at the moment was scouring pots for the cook and was quite dirty. He tried to excuse himself from coming into the room in such a mess, but the merchant made him come, and had a chair set for him. Dick began to think they must be making fun of him, so he begged them not to play tricks on a poor simple boy, but to let him go downstairs again back to his work in the kitchen.

"Indeed, Mr. Whittington," said the merchant, "we are all quite serious, and I most heartily rejoice at the news that these gentlemen have brought. For the captain has sold your cat to the King of Barbary, and brings you in return for her more riches than I possess in the whole world!"

Mr. Fitzwarren then told the men to open the great treasure they had brought with them, saying, "There is nothing more now for Mr. Whittington to do but to put it in some safe place."

Poor Dick hardly knew what to do. He begged his master to take what part of the fortune he pleased, since he owed it all to his kindness. "No, no," answered Mr. Fitzwarren, "this all belongs to you, and I have no doubt that you will use it well."

Dick next begged his mistress, and then Miss Alice, to accept a part of his good fortune, but they would not. At the same time they told him what great joy they felt at his great success. But he was far too kindhearted to keep it all to himself, so he made a present to the captain, the mate, and the rest of Mr. Fitzwarren's servants, and even to his old enemy, the cross cook.

After this Mr. Fitzwarren advised him to send for a tailor and get himself dressed like a gentleman, and told him he was welcome to live in his house till he could provide himself with a better place.

When Whittington's face was washed, his hair curled, and he was dressed in a smart suit of clothes, he was just as handsome and fine a young man as any who visited at Mr. Fitzwarren house. Fair Alice Fitzwarren, who had once been so kind to him and looked upon him with pity, now felt he was quite fit to be her sweetheart, especially because Whittington was always thinking what he could do to please her, and making her the prettiest presents that could be.

Mr. Fitzwarren saw their love for each other and soon proposed to unite them in marriage, and to this they both readily agreed. A day for the wedding was soon fixed; and they went along to church attended by the Lord Mayor, the court of aldermen, the sheriffs, and a great number of the richest merchants in London, whom they afterwards treated with a magnificent feast.

History tells us that Mr. Whittington and his lady lived in

great splendor, and were very happy. They had several children. He was sheriff, and three times made Lord Mayor of London, and received the honor of knighthood from King Henry the Fifth.

After the King's conquest of France, Sir Richard Whittington entertained him and the Queen at dinner at his mansion in so sumptuous a manner that the King said, "Never had I such a subject!" To which Sir Richard replied, "Never had I such a King."

THE BOGEY BEAST

THERE was once a woman who was very, very cheerful, though she had little to make her so, for she was old and poor and lonely. She lived in a little bit of a cottage and earned a scant living by running errands for her neighbors, getting a bite here and there as reward for her services. She always looked as spry and cheery as if she hadn't a want in the world.

Now one summer evening, as she was trotting full of smiles along the high road to her hovel, what should she see but a big black pot lying in the ditch.

"Goodness me!" she cried, "That would be the very thing for me if I only had something to put in it! Now who could have left it in the ditch?"

She looked about her expecting to see the owner nearby, but she could see nobody.

"Maybe there is a hole in it," she went on, "and that's why it has been cast away. But it would do fine to put a flower in for my window, so I'll just take it home with me."

With that she lifted the lid and looked inside. "Mercy me!" she cried. "If it isn't full of gold pieces. Here's luck!"

And so it was, full to the brim with great gold coins. Well, at first she simply stood stock-still, wondering if she was standing on her head or her heels. Then she began saying, "Laws! But I *do* feel rich. I feel awful rich!"

After she had said this many times, she began to wonder how she could get her treasure home. The pot was too heavy for her to carry, so she tied the end of her shawl to it and dragged it behind her like a cart.

"It will soon be dark," she said to herself as she trotted along. "So much the better! The neighbors won't see what I'm bringing home, and I shall have all the night to myself to think what I'll do! Perhaps I'll buy a grand house and just sit by the fire with a cup of tea and do no work at all like a queen. Or maybe I'll bury the pot in the garden and just keep a bit of gold in the old china teapot on the mantle. Goody! Goody! I feel so grand I don't recognize myself."

By this time she was a bit tired of dragging such a heavy weight and, stopping to rest a while, turned to look at her treasure.

And lo! It wasn't a pot of gold at all! It was nothing but a lump of silver.

She stared at it, and rubbed her eyes, and stared at it again.

"Well! I never!" she said at last. "And me thinking it was a pot of gold! I must have been dreaming. But this is luck! Silver is far less trouble—easier to watch over, and not so easily stolen. Those gold pieces would have been the death of me, and with this great lump of silver——"

So she went off again planning what she would do, and feeling as rich as rich, until becoming a bit tired again she stopped to rest and gave a look to see if her treasure was safe; and she saw nothing but a great lump of iron!

The Bogey Beast

"Well! I never!" said she again. "And I mistaking it for silver! I must have been dreaming. But this is luck! It's real convenient. I can get penny pieces for old iron, and penny pieces are handier for me than gold and silver. Why! I should never have slept a wink for fear of being robbed. But a penny piece comes in useful, and I shall sell that iron for a lot and be real rich—rolling rich."

So on she trotted full of plans as to how she would spend her penny pieces, till once more she stopped to rest and looked to see that her treasure was safe. And this time she saw nothing but a big stone.

"Well! I never!" she cried, full of smiles. "And to think I mistook it for iron. I must have been dreaming. But here's luck indeed, and me wanting a stone terribly bad to hold open the gate. Oh my! But this is a change for the better! It's a fine thing to have good luck."

So, all in a hurry to see how the stone would keep the gate open, she trotted off down the hill till she came to her own cottage. She unlatched the gate and then turned to unfasten her shawl from the stone which lay on the path behind her. Aye! It was still a stone, sure enough. There was plenty light to see it lying there, peaceable as a stone should.

She bent over it to unfasten the end of the shawl when— "Oh my!"

All of a sudden the stone gave a jump and a squeal, and in one moment was as big as a haystack. Then it let down four great lanky legs and threw out two long ears, flourished a great long tail and romped off, kicking and squealing and whinnying and laughing like a naughty, mischievous boy!

The Bogey Beast

The old woman stared after it till it was out of sight, then she burst out laughing too.

"Well!" she chuckled, "I am in luck! Quite the luckiest person hereabouts. Fancy my seeing the Bogey Beast all to myself and so close up too. My goodness! I do feel uplifted— that *GRAND!*"

So she went into her cottage and spent the evening chuckling over her good luck.

LITTLE RED RIDING HOOD

ONCE upon a time there was a little girl who was called little Red Riding Hood, because she was quite small and because she always wore a red cloak with a big red hood attached to it, which her grandmother had made for her.

Now one day her mother, who had been churning butter and baking cakes, said to her, "My dear, put on your red cloak with the hood, and take this cake and this pot of butter to your Grannie, and ask how she is, for I hear she is ailing."

Now little Red Riding Hood was very fond of her grandmother, who made her so many nice things, so she happily put on her cloak and started on her errand. But her grandmother lived some way off, and to reach the cottage little Red Riding Hood had to pass through a vast lonely forest. However, some woodcutters were at work in it, so little Red Riding Hood was not so very much alarmed when she saw a great big wolf coming toward her, because she knew that wolves were cowardly things.

And sure enough the wolf only stopped and asked her politely where she was going.

"I am going to see Grannie, take her this cake and this pot of butter, and ask how she is," said little Red Riding Hood.

"Does she live a very long way off?" asked the wolf craftily.

"Not so very far if you go by the straight road," replied

little Red Riding Hood. "You only have to pass the mill and the first cottage on the right is Grannie's; but I am going by the wood path because there are such a lot of nuts and flowers and butterflies."

"I wish you good luck," said the wolf politely. "Give my respects to your grandmother and tell her I hope she is quite well."

And with that he trotted off. But instead of going on his way he turned back, took the straight road to the old woman's cottage, and knocked at the door. Rap! Rap! Rap!

"Who's there?" asked the old woman, who was in bed.

"Little Red Riding Hood," sang out the wolf, making his voice as high as he could. "I've come to bring dear Grannie a pot of butter and a cake from mother, and to ask how you are."

"Pull the peg, and the latch will go up," said the old woman.

So the wolf pulled the peg, the latch went up, and—oh my!—it wasn't a minute before he had gobbled up old Grannie, for he had had nothing to eat for a week.

Then he shut the door, put on Grannie's nightcap, and, getting into bed, rolled himself up in the covers.

By and by along came little Red Riding Hood, who had been amusing herself by gathering nuts, running after butterflies, and picking flowers.

She knocked at the door. Rap! Rap! Rap!

"Who's there?" said the wolf, making his voice as soft as he could.

Now little Red Riding Hood could hear that the voice was

very gruff, but she thought her grandmother had a cold; so she said, "Little Red Riding Hood, with a pot of butter and a cake from mother, to ask how you are."

"Pull the peg, and the latch will go up."

So little Red Riding Hood pulled the peg, the latch went up, and there, she thought, was her grandmother in the bed, for the cottage was so dark she could not see well. The crafty wolf turned his face to the wall at first, made his voice as soft, as soft as he could, and said, "Come and kiss me, my dear."

Then little Red Riding Hood took off her cloak and went to the bed.

"Oh, Grandmamma, Grandmamma," said she. "What big arms you've got!"

"All the better to hug you with," said he.

"But, Grandmamma, Grandmamma, what big legs you have!"

"All the better to run with, my dear."

"Oh, Grandmamma, Grandmamma, what big ears you've got!"

"All the better to hear with, my dear."

"But, Grandmamma, Grandmamma, what big eyes you've got!"

"All the better to see you with, my dear!"

"Oh, Grandmamma, Grandmamma, what big teeth you've got!"

"All the better to eat you with, my dear!" said that wicked, wicked wolf, and with that he gobbled up little Red Riding Hood.

Feeling full and satisfied, the wolf curled up in Grannie's

bed and soon fell sound asleep. Just then, a woodcutter passing the house heard loud snoring and said to himself, "I must look in and see if there is anything the matter with the old lady."

So he went into the house and up to the bed, where he found the wolf fast asleep. He raised his up his ax to strike it when it occurred to him that perhaps the wolf had eaten up the old lady, and that she might still be saved. So he took out a knife and began to cut open the sleeping wolf. At the first little cut he saw the little red cloak, and in a moment the little girl sprang out, and cried, "Oh, how frightened I was, it was so dark inside the wolf!" Next old Grannie came out, alive, but hardly able to catch her breath.

The woodcutter brought some big stones to fill up the wolf, and when he woke up and tried to spring away the woodcutter dragged him back and he fell down dead.

Now they were all quite happy. The woodsman buried the wolf and went along home. Grannie ate the cake and butter which little Red Riding Hood had brought, and she soon felt much better. And little Red Riding Hood thought to herself, "I will always take the straight road from now on."

CHILDE ROWLAND

Childe Rowland and his brothers two
Were happily playing ball.
And their sister, Burd Helen, played
In the midst of them all.

For Burd Helen loved her brothers, and they loved her a good deal, too. At play she was always their companion and they cared for her as brothers should. And one day when they were playing ball close to the churchyard—

Childe Rowland kicked it with his foot
And caught it on the fly.
He gave the ball a mighty boot,
Which sent it to the sky.

Childe Rowland was Burd Helen's youngest brother and there was always a loving rivalry between them.

The ball had bounced to the right of the church, so, as Burd Helen ran to get it, she ran counter to the sun's course, and the light, shining full on her face, sent her shadow behind her. So, it happens at times when people forget and run against the light that their shadows are out of sight and cannot be taken care of properly.

Childe Rowland

What happened will be learned by and by; meanwhile, Burd Helen's three brothers waited for her return.

> And long they waited even through the rain,
> But she did not come back again.

Then they grew alarmed, and—

> They sought her east, they sought her west,
> They sought her up and down.
> And sad were the hearts of her brothers,
> Since she was nowhere to be found.

Not to be found anywhere—she had disappeared like dew on a May morning.

So at last her oldest brother went to Merlin the Magician, who could tell and foretell, see and foresee all things under the sun and beyond it, and asked him where Burd Helen could have gone.

"Fair Burd Helen," said the Magician, "must have been carried off with her shadow by the fairies when she was running round the church the wrong way, for fairies have power when people go against the light. She will now be in the Dark Tower of the King of Elfland, and only the boldest knight in the Kingdom will be able to bring her back."

"If it is possible to bring her back," said the oldest brother, "I will do it, or I will die in the attempt."

"It is possible," said Merlin the Magician gravely. "But

woe be to the man or mother's son who attempts the task if he does not know beforehand what he must do."

Now the oldest brother of fair Burd Helen was brave and danger did not dismay him, so he begged the Magician to tell him exactly what he should do, as he was determined to go and find his sister. And the Great Magician told him and after he had learned his lessons, he buckled on his sword, said good-bye to his brothers and his mother, and set out for the Dark Tower of Elfland to bring Burd Helen back.

> But they waited long, and longer still,
> They suffered with the pain.
> And sad were the hearts of his brothers,
> For he came not back again.

So after a time Burd Helen's second brother went to Merlin the Magician and said, "Show me, for I go to find my brother and sister in the Dark Tower of the King of Elfland and bring them back." For he also was brave and danger did not dismay him.

Then when he had been well trained and had learned his lessons, he said good-bye to Childe Rowland, his brother, and to his mother the good Queen, he strapped on his sword, and set out for the Dark Tower of Elfland to bring back Burd Helen and her brother.

Now when they had waited and waited a long, long time, and none had come back from the Dark Tower of Elfland, Childe Rowland, the youngest, the best beloved of Burd Helen's brothers, asked his mother to let him also go on the quest; for he was the bravest of them all, and neither death nor danger could dismay him. At first his mother the Queen said, "No! You are the last of my children; if you are lost, all is lost!"

But he begged so hard that finally the good Queen his mother wished him luck and buckled about his waist his father's sword and as she tied it on she chanted the victory spell.

So Childe Rowland said good-bye and went to the cave of the Great Magician Merlin.

"Yet once more, Master," said the youth, "and tell me how I may find fair Burd Helen and her two brothers in the Dark Tower of Elfland."

"My son," replied Merlin, "there are two things; they may seem simple but they are hard to perform. One thing is to be done and the other must not be done. Now the first thing you have to do is this: after you have entered the Land of Faery, *whoever speaks to you,* you must cut off his head. In this you must not fail. The next thing you must *not* do is this: after you have entered the Land of Faery, neither eat nor drink, for if in Elfland you drink one drop or eat one bite, you will never again see Middle Earth."

Then Childe Rowland said these two lessons over and over until he knew them by heart; then he thanked the Great Master and went on his way to find the Dark Tower of Elfland.

And he traveled far and fast, until at last on a wide moor he came upon a herd of horses feeding, and the horses were wild, and their eyes were like coals of fire.

Then he knew they must be the horses of the King of Elfland and that at last he was in the Land of Faery.

Childe Rowland

So Childe Rowland said to the herdsman, "Can you tell me where to find the Dark Tower of the Elfland King?"

And the herdsman answered, "No, that is beyond me, but go a little farther and you will come to a herdsman tending his cows who may be able to tell you."

Then at once Childe Rowland drew his father's sword and cut off the herdsman's head, so that it rolled on the moor and frightened the King of Elfland's horses. Then he traveled farther till he came to a wide pasture where a herdsman was tending his cows. And the cows looked at him with fiery eyes, so he knew that they must be the King of Elfland's cows, and that he was still in the Land of Faery. Then he said to the herdsman, "Can you tell me where to find the Dark Tower of the Elfland King?"

And the herdsman answered, "No, that is beyond me; but go a little farther and you will come to a woman who keeps chickens who may tell you."

So Childe Rowland, remembering his lesson, took out his sword and off went the herdsman's head spinning among the grasses and frightening the King of Elfland's cows.

Then he traveled farther till he came to an orchard where an old woman in a gray cloak was feeding chickens. And the chickens' little eyes were like little coals of fire, so he knew that they were the King of Elfland's chickens, and that he was still in the Land of Faery.

And he said to her, "Can you tell me where to find the Dark Tower of the King of Elfland?"

Now the old woman looked at him and smiled. "Surely I can tell you," she said. "Go on a little farther. There you will find a low green hill; green and low against the sky. And the hill will have three terrace-rings upon it from bottom to top. Go round the first terrace and say:

'Open from within;
Let me in! Let me in!'

Then go round the second terrace and say:

'Open wide, open wide;
Let me inside.'

Then go round the third terrace and say:

'Open fast, open fast;
Let me in at last.'

Then a door will open and let you into the Dark Tower of the King of Elfland. Only remember to go round counter to the sun. If you go round with the sun the door will not open. So good luck to you!''

Now she spoke so honestly, and smiled so frankly, that Childe Rowland forgot for a moment what he had to do. Therefore he thanked the old woman for her courtesy and was just going on, when, all of a sudden, he remembered his lesson. And he took out his sword and cut off the old woman's head, so that it rolled among the corn and frightened the fiery-eyed chickens of the King of Elfland.

After that he went on and on, till, against the blue sky, he saw a round green hill set with three terraces from top to bottom.

Then he did as the old woman had told him, not forgetting to go round the wrong way, so that the sun was always on his face.

Now when he had gone round the third terrace saying:

"Open fast, open fast;
Let me in at last,"

what should happen but that he should see a door in the hill-side. And it opened and let him in. Then it closed behind him with a click, and Childe Rowland was left in the dark, for he had gotten at last to the Dark Tower of the King of Elfland.

It was very dark at first, perhaps because the sun had blinded his eyes, but after a while, it became twilight, though where the light came from none could tell, unless through the walls and the roof, for there were neither windows nor candles. But in the dim light he could see a long passage of rough arches made of rock that was transparent and all encrusted with silver and many bright stones. And the air was warm, so he went on and on in the twilight that came from nowhere, until he found himself before two wide doors barred with iron. But they flew open at his touch and he saw a wonderful, large, and spacious hall that seemed to him to be as long and as broad as the green hill itself. The roof was supported by pillars wide and lofty beyond the pillars of a cathedral, and they were made of gold and silver, and between and around them were woven wreaths of flowers. And the flowers were of diamonds and topaz and the leaves of emerald. And the arches met in the middle of the roof where there was hung, by a golden chain, an immense lamp made of a hollowed pearl, white and translucent. And in the middle of this lamp was a mighty jewel, blood-red, that kept spinning round and round, shedding its light to the very ends of the huge hall, which seemed to be filled with the shining of the setting sun.

At one end of the hall, was a marvelous, wondrous, glorious couch of velvet, and silk, and gold; and on it sat fair Burd Helen combing her beautiful golden hair with a golden comb. But her face looked pale, as if it were made of stone. And when she saw Childe Rowland she never moved and her voice sounded like the voice of the dead.

At first Childe Rowland felt he must clasp this semblance of his dear sister in his arms; but he remembered the lesson which the Great Magician Merlin had taught him and drawing his sword and turning his eyes from the horrible sight, he struck with all his might at the enchanted form of Burd Helen.

But when he turned to look in fear and trembling, there she was herself. And she clasped him in her arms and cried:

> "Oh, hear you this, my youngest brother,
>   Why didn't you stay at home?
>   Had you a hundred thousand lives,
>   You couldn't spare one!
>
> "But sit you down, my dearest dear,
>   Oh! woe that you were born,

Childe Rowland

For, when the King of Elfland comes,
Your future will be torn."

So with tears and smiles she sat beside him on the couch, and they told each other what they each had suffered and done. He told her how he had come to Elfland, and she told him how she had been carried off, shadow and all, because she ran round a church the wrong way, and how her brothers had been enchanted, and lay entombed as if dead, as she had been, because they had not had the courage to obey the Great Magician's lesson to the letter, and cut off her head.

Now after a time Childe Rowland, who had traveled far and fast, became very hungry, and forgetting all about the second lesson of the Magician Merlin, asked his sister for some food. And she, being still under the spell of Elfland, could not warn him of his danger; she could only look at him sadly as she rose up and brought him a golden basin full of bread and milk.

Now in those days it was manners before taking food from anyone to say thank you with your eyes, and so just as Childe Rowland was about to put the golden bowl to his lips, he raised his eyes to his sister's.

And in an instant he remembered what the Great Magician had said.

So he smashed the bowl on the ground, and standing square and strong he cried like a challenge, "I will drink nothing and eat nothing until fair Burd Helen is set free."

Then immediately there was a loud noise like thunder, and the folding doors of the vast hall burst open and the King of Elfland entered like a storm of wind. What he was really like

Childe Rowland

Childe Rowland had no time to see, for with a bold cry he said "Strike your hardest if you dare!" as he rushed to meet the foe, his good sword in his hand.

And Childe Rowland and the King of Elfland fought and fought and fought, while Burd Helen, with her hands clasped, watched them in fear and hope.

So they fought and fought and fought, until at last Childe Rowland beat the King of Elfland to his knees. And the King cried, "I yield. You have beaten me in a fair fight."

Then Childe Rowland said, "I grant you mercy if you will release my sister and my brothers from all spells and enchantments and let us go back to Middle Earth."

So that was agreed; and the Elfin King went to a golden chest and he took a vial that was filled with a blood-red liquor. And with this liquor he anointed the ears and the eyelids, the nostrils, the lips, and the fingertips of the bodies of Burd Helen's two brothers who lay as if dead in two golden caskets.

And immediately they sprang to life and declared that their souls only had been away, but had now returned.

After this the Elfin King said a charm which took away the very last bit of enchantment, and down the huge hall that showed as if it were lit by the setting sun, and through the long passage of rough arches made of rock that was transparent and all encrusted with silver and many bright stones, where twilight reigned, the brothers and their sister passed. Then the door opened in the green hill, it clicked behind them, and they left the Dark Tower of the King of Elfland never to return.

For no sooner were they in the light of day, than they found themselves at home.

But fair Burd Helen was careful never to go the wrong way round a church again.

CAPORUSHES

ONCE upon a time, a long, long while ago, when all the world was young and all sorts of strange things happened, there lived a very rich gentleman whose wife had died leaving him three lovely daughters whom he loved dearly.

Now one day he wanted to find out if they loved him in return, so he said to the eldest, "How much do you love me, my dear?"

And she answered quickly, "As I love my life."

"Very good, my dear," said he, and gave her a kiss. Then he said to the second girl, "How much do you love me, my dear?"

And she answered as swift as thought, "Better than all the world."

"Good!" he replied, and patted her on the cheek. Then he turned to the youngest, who was also the prettiest.

"And how much do *you* love me, my dearest?"

Now the youngest daughter was not only pretty, she was clever. So she thought a moment, then she said slowly, "I love you as fresh meat loves salt!"

Now when her father heard this he was very angry, because he really loved her more than the others.

"What!" he said. "If that is all you give me in return for all

Caporushes

I've given you, out of my house you go." There and then he turned her out of the home where she had been born and bred, and shut the door in her face.

Not knowing where to go, she wandered on and she wandered on, till she came to a big meadow where the reeds grew tall and the rushes swayed in the wind like a field of corn. There she sat down and braided herself a coverall of rushes and a cap to match, so as to hide her fine clothes and her beautiful golden hair that was set with milk-white pearls. For she was a wise girl, and thought that in such lonely country some robber might harm her to get her fine clothes and jewels.

It took a long time to make the dress and cap, and while she braided she sang a little song:

> "Hide my hair, O cap o' rushes,
> Hide my heart, O robe o' rushes.
> Sure! my answer had no fault,
> I love him more than he loves salt."

And the meadow birds sat and listened and sang back to her:

> "Cap o' rushes, shed no tear,
> Robe o' rushes, have no fear;
> With these words if fault he'd find,
> Sure your father must be blind."

When her task was finished she put on her robe of rushes and it hid all her fine clothes, and she put on the cap and it hid all her beautiful hair, so that she looked like an ordinary country girl. But the birds flew away, singing as they flew:

"Cap-o-rushes! we can see,
　Robe o' rushes! what you be,
　Fair and clean, and fine and tidy,
　So you'll be whate'er betide ye."

By this time she was very hungry, so she wandered on and she wandered on, until just at sunset she came upon a great house on the edge of the meadow. It had a fine front door, but remembering her dress of rushes she went around to the back. And there she saw a fat kitchen maid washing pots and pans with a very sulky face. Being a clever girl, she guessed what the maid was wanting, and said, "If I may have a night's lodging, I will scrub the pots and pans for you."

"Why! Here's luck," replied the kitchen maid. "I was just wanting to go walking with my sweetheart. So if you will do my work you shall share my bed and have a bite of my supper. Only mind you, scrub the pots clean or the cook will be at me."

The next morning the pots were scraped so clean that they looked like new, and the saucepans were polished like silver, and the cook said to the kitchen maid, "Who cleaned these pots? Not you, I'll swear." The maid had to confess the truth. The cook was ready to fire the old maid and put on the new, but the girl would not hear of it.

"The maid was kind to me and gave me a night's lodging,"

189

she said. "So now I will stay without pay and do the dirty work for her."

So Caporushes—for so they called her since she would give no other name—stayed on and cleaned the pots and scraped the saucepans.

Now it so happened that the master's son came of age, and to celebrate the occasion a ball was given for the wealthy neighbors, for the young man was a grand dancer. It was a very fine party, and after supper was served, the servants were allowed to go and watch the dancers from the gallery of the ballroom.

But Caporushes refused to go, for she also was a grand dancer and she was afraid that when she heard the fiddles starting a merry jig she might start dancing. She excused herself by saying she was too tired from scraping pots and washing saucepans, and when the others went off, she crept up to her bed.

But alas and alack-a-day! The door had been left open, and as she lay in her bed she could hear the fiddlers fiddling away and the tramp of dancing feet.

Then she got up and removed her cap and robe of rushes, and there she was ever so fine and tidy. She was in the ballroom in a moment joining in the jig, and none was more beautiful or better dressed than she. As for her dancing . . . ! The master's son singled her out at once, and with a fine bow engaged her as his partner for the rest of the night. So she danced away to her heart's content, while the whole room was agog, trying to find out who the beautiful young stranger could be. But she kept her own counsel and, making some excuse, slipped away before the ball finished. When her fellow-servants came to bed, there she was in hers in her cap and robe of rushes, pretending to be fast asleep.

Next morning, however, the maids could talk of nothing but the beautiful stranger.

"You should have seen her," they said. "She was the loveliest young lady you ever saw, not a bit like the likes of us. Her golden hair was silvered with pearls, and her dress! You wouldn't believe how she was dressed. The young master never took his eyes off her."

And Caporushes only smiled and said, with a twinkle in her eye, "I should like to see her, but I don't think I ever shall."

"Oh yes, you will," they replied, "for the young master has ordered another ball tonight in hopes she will come to dance again."

But that evening Caporushes refused once more to go to the gallery, saying she was too tired with cleaning pots and scraping saucepans. And once more when she heard the fiddlers fiddling she said to herself, "I must have one dance—just one with the young master for he dances so beautifully." She felt certain he would dance with her.

And sure enough, when she had removed her cap and robe of rushes and entered the ballroom, there he was at the door waiting for her, for he had determined to dance with no one else.

He took her by the hand, and they danced down the ballroom. It was a sight of all sights! Never were there such dancers —so young, so handsome, so fine!

But once again Caporushes kept her own counsel and just

in time slipped away on some excuse, so that when her fellow-servants came to their beds they found her in hers, pretending to be fast asleep; but her cheeks were all flushed and her breath came fast. So they said, "She is dreaming. We hope her dreams are happy."

But next morning they were full of what she had missed. Never was there such a beautiful young gentleman as the young master! Never was there such a beautiful young lady! Never was there such beautiful dancing! Everyone else had stopped dancing to look on.

And Caporushes, with a twinkle in her eyes, said, "I should like to see her; but I'm *sure* I never shall!"

"Oh yes!" they replied. "If you come tonight you're sure to see her, for the young master has ordered another ball in hopes the beautiful stranger will come again, for it's easy to see he is madly in love with her."

Then Caporushes told herself she would not dance again, since it was not fit for a young master to be in love with his kitchen maid. But, alas! The moment she heard the fiddlers fiddling, she removed her rushes, and there she was fine and tidy as ever! She didn't even have to brush her beautiful golden hair! And once again she was in the ballroom in a moment, dancing away with the young master, who never took his eyes off her, and implored her to tell him who she was. But she kept her own counsel and only told him that she never, never, never would come to dance anymore, and that he must say good-bye. And he held her hand so tightly that she had to struggle to get away and, lo and behold! His ring came off his finger, and as she ran up to her bed there it was in her hand!

Caporushes

She had just time to put on her cap and robe of rushes, when her fellow-servants came trooping in and found her awake.

"It was the noise you made coming upstairs," she said. But they said, "Not we! It is the whole place that is in an uproar searching for the beautiful stranger. The young master tried to detain her, but she slipped away from him like an eel. But he declares he will find her, for if he doesn't he will die of love for her."

Then Caporushes laughed. "Young men don't die of love," she said. "He will find someone else."

But he didn't. He spent his whole time looking for his beautiful dancer, but go where he might and ask whom he would, he never heard anything about her. And day by day he grew thinner and thinner and paler and paler, until at last he took to his bed.

And the housekeeper came to the cook and said, "Cook the nicest dinner you can cook, for the young master eats nothing."

The cook made soups and jellies and puddings and roast chicken and gravy; but the young man would eat none of them.

And Caporushes cleaned the pots and scraped the saucepans and said nothing.

Then the housekeeper came crying and said to the cook, "Prepare some broth for the young master. Perhaps he'll take that. If not he will die for love of the beautiful dancer. If she could see him now she would have pity on him."

So the cook began to make the broth, and Caporushes stopped scraping the saucepans and watched her.

Caporushes

"Let me stir it," she said, "while you fetch a cup from the pantry."

So Caporushes stirred the broth, and what did she do but slip the young master's ring into it before the cook came back!

Then the butler took the cup upstairs on a silver tray. But when the young master saw it he waved it away, till the butler with tears begged him just to taste it.

So the young master took a silver spoon and stirred the broth; and he felt something hard at the bottom of the cup. When he fished it up, lo! it was his own ring! Then he sat up in bed and said quite loud, "Send for the cook!"

When she came he asked her who had made the broth.

"I did," she said, for she was half pleased and half frightened.

Then he looked at her all over and said, "No, you didn't! You're too stout! Tell me who made it and you shall not be harmed!"

The cook began to cry. "If you please, sir, I *did* make it, but Caporushes stirred it."

"And who is Caporushes?" asked the young man.

"If you please, sir, Caporushes is the kitchenmaid," whimpered the cook.

The young man sighed and fell back on his pillow. "Send Caporushes here," he said in a faint voice, for he really was very near dying.

When Caporushes came he looked at her cap and her robe of rushes and turned his face to the wall, but he asked her in a weak little voice, "From whom did you get that ring?"

Now when Caporushes saw the poor young man so weak

and worn with love for her, her heart melted, and she replied softly, "From him that gave it me," said she, and took off her cap and robe of rushes, and there she was as fine and tidy as ever with her beautiful golden hair all silvered over with pearls.

The young man caught sight of her out of the corner of his eye, and sat up in bed and drew her to him and gave her a great big kiss.

So, of course, they were to be married in spite of her being only a kitchenmaid, for she told no one who she was. Everyone far and near was asked to the wedding. Among the invited guests was Caporushes' father, who, from grief at losing his favorite daughter, had lost his sight, and was very dull and miserable. However, as a friend of the family, he had to come to the young master's wedding.

The marriage feast was to be the finest ever seen; but Caporushes went to her friend the cook and said, "Make every dish without one bit of salt."

"That'll be very unpleasant," replied the cook, but because she prided herself on having let Caporushes stir the broth and so saved the young master's life, she did as she was asked, and made every dish for the wedding breakfast without one bit of salt.

Now when the company sat down to table their faces were full of smiles and happiness, for all the dishes looked so nice and tasty. But no sooner had the guests begun to eat than their faces fell, for nothing can be tasty without salt.

Then Caporushes' blind father, whom his daughter had seated next to her, burst out crying.

"What is the matter?" she asked.

Caporushes

Then the old man sobbed, "I had a daughter whom I loved dearly, dearly. And I asked her how much she loved me, and she replied, 'As fresh meat loves salt.' I was angry with her and turned her out of house and home, for I thought she didn't love me at all. But now I see she loved me best of all."

As he said the words his eyes were opened, and there beside him was his daughter lovelier than ever.

She gave him one hand, and her husband, the other, and laughed saying, "I love you both as fresh meat loves salt." And after that they were all happy forever more.

THE RED ETTIN

THERE was once a widow who lived on a small bit of ground, which she rented from a farmer. The widow had two sons, and by and by it was time to send them away to seek their fortune. One day she told her eldest son to take a can and bring her water from the well, that she might bake a cake for him. However much or however little water he brought, the cake would be great or small accordingly. That cake would be all that she could give him when he went on his travels.

The lad went away to the well, and filled the can with water, but the can had a hole in it and the most part of the water had run out before he got back. So his cake was very small. Small as it was, his mother asked him if he was willing to take half of it with her blessing, telling him that if he chose to take the whole cake he would get only her curse. The young man, thinking he might have to travel a long way, and not knowing when or how he might get other provisions, said he would like to have the whole cake, despite his mother's curse. She gave him the whole cake, and her curse along with it. Then he took his brother aside, and gave him a knife to keep till he should come back, asking him to look at it every morning. As long as the knife remained shiny, then he might be sure that its owner was well; but if the knife grew dim and rusty, then for certain some ill had befallen him.

So the young man went out to seek his fortune. He went all that day and all the next day and on the third day, in the afternoon, he came to where a shepherd was sitting with a flock of sheep. He went up to the shepherd and asked him to whom the sheep belonged, and the shepherd answered:

"To the Red Ettin of Ireland
    Who lives in Ballygan,
    He stole King Malcolm's daughter,
    The king of fair Scotland.
    And every day he strikes her
    With a bright silver wand.
    'Tis said there's one predestined
    To be his mortal foe;
    But sure that man is not yet born,
    And long may it be so!"

After this the shepherd told him to beware of the beasts he should meet next, for they were a very different from any he had seen before.

So the young man went on, and by and by he saw a horde of dreadful, terrible, horrible beasts, with two heads, and on every head four horns! He was so frightened that he ran away as fast as he could, until he came to a castle that stood on a hill, with the door standing wide open. He went into the castle for shelter, and there he saw an old woman sitting beside the kitchen fire. He asked if he might stay for the night, as he was tired from a long journey. The old woman said he might, but it was not a good place for him to rest, as the castle belonged to the Red Ettin, who was a very terrible monster with three heads, who spared no living man it could get hold of. The young man would have gone away, but he was afraid of the two-headed four-horned beasts outside. He begged the old woman to hide him as best she could, and not tell the Ettin he was there. He thought, if he could rest for the night, he might get away in the morning without meeting with the dreadful, terrible, horrible beasts. So the old woman tucked him in with a blanket in a closet under the stairs.

But he had not been long in his hiding place, when the awful Ettin came in. And no sooner was he in, than he cried:

"Snouk but! and snouk ban!
I smell the smell of an earthly man;
Be he living, or be he dead,
His heart this night shall be my bread."

Well, the monster began to search about, and he soon found the poor young man and pulled him from his hiding-place. And when he had got him out, he told him that if he could answer three questions his life should be spared.

The monster's first head asked, "A thing without an end; what's that?"

But the young man knew not.

Then the second head asked, "The smaller the more dangerous; what's that?"

But the young man knew not.

And then the third head asked, "The dead carrying the living? Answer me that."

But the young man knew not.

So the Red Ettin took a mallet from behind the door, knocked the lad on the head, and turned him into a pillar of stone.

Now on the morning after this happened the younger brother took out the knife to look at it, and he was sad to find it all brown with rust. He told his mother that the time had come for him to go away upon his travels also. At first she refused to let him go; but at last she told him to take the can to the well for water, that she might make a cake for him. So he went, but as he was bringing home the water, a raven flying over his head cried to him to look, and he would see that the water was running out through a hole in the can. Now being a young man of sense, and seeing the water running out, he took some clay and patched up the hole, so that he brought home enough water to bake a large cake. And when his mother told him to take half the cake with her blessing, he took it instead of taking the whole with her curse.

He went away on his journey with his mother's blessing. After he had traveled a far way, he met an old woman who asked him if he would give her a bit of his cake. And he said, "I will gladly do that"; and he gave her a piece of the cake. Then the old woman, who was really a fairy, gave him a magic wand that might help him, if he used it properly. She told him a great deal that would happen to him, and what he ought to do in all circumstances. After that, she vanished in an instant. He went on his way until he came up to the old man who was herding the sheep; and when he asked him to whom the sheep belonged, the answer was:

> "To the Red Ettin of Ireland
> Who lives in Ballygan,
> He stole King Malcolm's daughter,
> The king of fair Scotland.
> And every day he strikes her
> With a bright silver wand.
> But now I fear his end is near,
> And death is close at hand;
> For you're to be, I plainly see,
> The heir of all his land."

The younger brother went on his way, but when he came to the place where the dreadful, terrible, horrible beasts were standing, he did not stop nor run away, but boldly waded through them. When one came up roaring with open mouth to devour him, he struck it with his wand, and laid it in an instant dead at his feet. He soon came to the Ettin's castle, where he found the door shut, but he knocked boldly and was admitted. The old woman who sat by the fire warned him of the terrible Ettin, and told him about the fate of his brother; but he was not to be afraid, and would not even hide.

By and by the monster came in, crying as before:

> "Snouk but! and snouk ban!
> I smell the smell of an earthly man;

The Red Ettin

Be he living, or be he dead,
His heart this night shall be my bread."

He saw the young man, and told him to stand up and answer three questions if he wished to live.

So the monster's first head asked, "What's the thing without an end?"

Now the younger brother had been told by the fairy what he ought to say, so he answered, "A bowl."

The first head frowned, but the second head asked, "The smaller the more dangerous; what's that?"

"A bridge," said the younger brother, quite fast.

The first and the second heads frowned, but the third head asked, "When does the dead carry the living? Answer me that."

At this the young man answered at once and said, "When a ship sails on the sea with men inside her."

When the Red Ettin found all his riddles answered, he knew that his power was gone. He tried to run away, but the young man took up an axe and whacked off the monster's three heads. Then he asked the old woman to show him where the king's daughter was kept. The old woman took him upstairs, and opened a great many doors, and out of every door came a beautiful lady who had been imprisoned there by the Red Ettin. Last of all the ladies was the king's daughter. Then the old woman took him down into a low room, and there stood a stone pillar; but he had only to touch it with his wand, and his brother came to life.

All of the prisoners were overjoyed at their deliverance, for which they thanked the younger brother again and again. The next day they all set out for the king's court, and a gallant company they made. The king married his daughter to the young man who had delivered her, and married a noble's daughter to his brother.

So they all lived happily all the rest of their days.